T0366919

THE KID

JOHN SEELYE

THE KID

University of Nebraska Press
Lincoln and London

First Bison Book printing: October 1982

Library of Congress Cataloging in Publication Data
Seelye, John D.
   The kid.
   Reprint. originally published: New York : Viking Press, c1972.
   "A Bison book."
   I.   Title.
[PS3569.E35K5   1982]   813'.54   82-6998
ISBN 0-8032-9131-0 (pbk.)   AACR2

Published by arrangement with the author

For Leslie Fiedler

Sunt . . . nobis . . . Haedorumque dies servandi.

— VIRGIL

The old days, the happy days, when
Wyoming was a Territory with a future
instead of a State with a past, and
the unfenced cattle grazed upon her
ranges by prosperous thousands. . . .

— OWEN WISTER

I heard, four years ago, that he was
justice of the peace in a remote village
in Montana, and was a good citizen and
greatly respected.

— MARK TWAIN

To understand the West as somehow a
joke comes a little closer to getting
it straight.

— LESLIE FIEDLER

THE KID

I

I didn't see them ride into town but there was a man who did, Shirey Monahan, who was taking his team into Douglas to pick up feed for his store. Shire raised them outside of town, on the flats, where they was coming from the east, and he remembered them on account of their mules. Plenty of riders had come up that road in the last few weeks, mostly cowpunchers looking for work, but there hadn't been nobody else on a mule, so Shire took special note of them two strangers. He reckoned they had been riding a long ways, because the mules had their legs and bellies slathered with red muck, so thick you couldn't tell where the animal left off and the man begun. The both of them was slumped down in their saddles, plumb wore out. Shire couldn't make out their faces on account of they had the collars of their sheepskins up and their hats pulled down over their ears from the morning cold. Besides, the sun was just coming up behind them and their fronts was mostly shadows and steam from their breath. They didn't say nothing when Shire went by, and he didn't neither.

It was late April then, back in '87, but the weather was still plenty raw and cold. That had been the worst winter ever, and the Laramie peaks was still white away off past the southern foothills, bone white and sharp as a grizzly's teeth against that bitter cold morning blue. There was considerable snow left even on the flats, patches of snow and patches of dead cows. Poor critters. There was coulees where you could find a dozen or more all heaped together, where they had crowded to keep warm, starved and bloated and black, just pitiful to look at. Now and then you thought you saw one of them move, but when you rode over to check you found it was only a buzzard tugging at something loose. And magpies and crows had a gay time, too, calling back and forth at each other about the good things they was finding. The sky was full of birds going crazy trying to make up their minds where to start their next meal. *They* was having a good year, I reckon.

Some cows was left standing, but that was about the only difference betwixt them and the dead ones. They kept together mostly, like the others, and you could see there wasn't a spoonful of spunk left amongst them. A cow ain't like a horse, you know, and never does have much spirit, just stubbornness, and after what them poor brutes had been through even that was in mighty short supply. It did seem like all they had left was scaredness, and what was keeping them standing was the fear of lying down. They was easily spooked, and nothing more than the flap of a buzzard's wing could set a bunch of them moving, gallumphing along in that slack-kneed way a wore-out steer has of running, one or two maybe going down on their knees and then all the way down, laying there panting, eyes stuck out and their tongues lolling, scared nearly to death and sometimes all the way.

We was all scared, back then, and a great many ranch owners done just what their cows was doing, laid down and called it quits. You see, it *had* been boom times, and everybody had been putting every cent they owned or owed into cows and more cows, thinking it wasn't ever going to end. People down in Texas kept driving their stock north to fatten in Wyoming and Montana, and as soon as they was up to size, the U.P. would haul them away to the Eastern yards, where they was cut up into sirloins, T-bones, porterhouse, and all the rest that city people was hungering for, from the tenderloins down to tripes. Beef seemed a sure thing, and unless the nation went vegetarian, it looked like a lot of men was going to get as rich as some men already had.

Then, in '85, the market slumped a bit on account of there being more cows than people willing to eat them, and profits was cut back considerable. That winter was a bad one, and the summer of '86 wasn't no better, so hot and dry that the forage withered up before it had any growth to it. There was dust everywhere, so thick around the herds you had to take it on faith any cows was inside the cloud. Faith was all most ranchers had left by then, and they held regular prayer meetings, sitting around telling each other that the slump was a good thing because it and the bad weather would drive a lot of the come-lately, easy-dollar men out, and that beef was as good as bullion as soon as the market evened off at a reasonable profit, say forty to fifty per cent. Just wait till next spring, they kept saying. Well, it was a long wait.

Because the snow begun early that year, in November, and it just never stopped. For a time the wind kept the high ground clear, but there wasn't much grass left up there anyhow, and pretty soon even that was gone. One long blizzard it was, the snow drifting so deep you couldn't get hay out to the cattle, if you had hay, and most ranchers didn't. They had reckoned on it being cheaper to lose a few head every winter than to lay in feed. Here and there some of the cows would bunch together and straggle in from the range to where the rancher lived, and about drive him and his men loco with their bawling, because there wasn't nothing to feed them and nowheres to hide from

5

that awful sound, which was far worse than the moaning and groaning of the blizzard. They had to board up their windows, even, to keep the cows from busting in, and when spring finally come they found dead cows in every shed and lean-to, where they had crowded to keep alive.

Then, in January, a chinook blew in, which was a warm southern wind ranchers counted on most winters to keep the snow melting so their stock could paw down to graze. But the snow was too deep for any chinook, and it only melted enough so that when cold weather come back it froze into solid ice. The creeks was frozen too, and probably as many cows died from thirst as was starved to death. Then the snow started again, and the cows done the only thing they can do in such cases, which is to stand still with their rumps to the wind. And when they couldn't stand no longer they lay down, and when whatever it is keeps a cow alive gave out, they died. And still the snow kept falling, the wind packing it down and covering all the dead animals except here and there you could see a horn or a head or maybe a leg sticking up in the air. They tell me two-thirds of the stock in Wyoming was killed off that year, and things wasn't no better in Montana.

By late March the snow begun to melt off the dead cows so you could take a head count, and it was plain that there wasn't much left to round up. The market was still lower than a snake's hips, and so was the ranchers. A number just drifted away, and those that stayed cut expenses to the bone, which meant a lot of punchers got trimmed from the payroll. It took a while for the boys to catch on, riding from ranch to ranch, looking for jobs which just wasn't there, because a cowboy has got a good deal of the cow in him, rubbed off as you might say, like the smell, and it sometimes takes a sledge hammer to per-suade him of something. So these punchers kept wandering about, looking for work even though they could see there wasn't none to be had. Not a one of them seemed to have any cash money, and a cowboy's credit is something short of a whore's reputation, so it wasn't long before they was living off the pure Western air. Which will give you the colic, you know, and make the neighborhood riper than some of them Yellowstone springs.

So there we was in Fort Besterman, Wyoming Territory, in the spring of '87, with nothing to do except watch the town fill up with colicky cowboys, all sore as a boil and convicted that somebody had dealt them a bum hand. A few punchers blamed the weather, naturally, but nobody paid them much note. Most was looking for people to blame—other people—and the punchers who got the biggest audience was those with the most generous views, namely the ones that blamed the Association and the Government. They claimed the Association hadn't no right letting things go bust, and it was the Government's fault for letting them get away with it. If the cows was all dead, it wasn't the punchers' fault, and they shouldn't have to starve just because the cows had. There was plenty more dogies in Texas, everybody knew that, hundreds and thousands of them, and if the ranchers wasn't going to do nothing but sit around whimpering with their asses in a crack, why, the Government ought to pass a law to get those Texas steers moving north. As soon as the people in the East saw we meant business, why, the price of cows would soar, because it was only being kept down by the big beef interests which was hoping to break our backs.

It was mostly talk, but you could feel the tightness just the same, like a clock that's got something wrong with it and won't run. You can wind it up, but that's all, and every day you wind it a little tighter hoping maybe it will start and begin to unwind, but it don't, and you know that sooner or later the damn thing will go "whang!" and unwind one hell of a lot faster than you wanted it to.

What made things particularly bad was that the only cowpunchers hanging around town was the stubborn ones and those without no sense. The ones with brains headed for Douglas and the rail spur, because an empty boxcar was the best

7

chance for anybody who could see how things was going, how there wasn't to be no hiring that year or maybe ever again. What we was stuck with was the remains, so to speak, those that was either the dumbest or the thick-headedest or the poorest. And worst of all was the fear. Under all that big talk you knowed there wasn't no difference betwixt them cowboys and the cows, only the cows showed it by standing around shivering while the cowboys stood around bellyaching.

And drinking.

Because when a puncher is down to his last inch of tin, he cuts back on frills and sticks to essentials. Which means he stops eating and keeps on drinking. There was a number of saloons in Besterman at that time, but the cowboys' favorite was Jake Bradley's place, because Bradley would sell whiskey on account. On account of he started out that way and then the boys wouldn't let him stop. Anybody wanting to take a tally of broke punchers in Besterman only had to go down to Bradley's at eight in the morning and count the heads standing outside on the boardwalk.

Now cowpunchers as a rule is pretty good fellers, full of horseplay and jokes, but this bunch outside Bradley's was ornery as a constipated bull. Hard times done it, and being out of work, for nothing makes a puncher more restless than having nothing to do. Before, when they had jobs, coming to town meant drinking and whoring and generally raising hell, having a good time for a couple days until their money was spent or stole and they could get back to work. That's all town was good for, a place to get broke in fast, so they could get back to punching cows. But here they was dead broke and getting broker, stuck with town and more town, and it wasn't fun no more because there wasn't no work at the end of the run. Just more town.

But they kept at it, out of habit, I reckon, as much as hope, showing up every morning and standing around waiting for Bradley to open up, and if he didn't open at eight o'clock sharp, they begun to make noise. The gist of the noise was that if Bradley didn't open up right then and there they'd enlarge the entrance considerable. Well, Bradley maybe was a minute or so late every now and then because of his wife keeping him upstairs with a little of her marvelous hindsight on how dumb he had been ever to give cowboys credit in the first place, but he wasn't ever very late, so they left his architecture alone.

Well, caught like he was betwixt his wife and them thirsty, broke, ornery cowboys, Bradley didn't much admire his situation. He told the Captain he was going to close down. He said he wasn't no cowboy hisself and therefore couldn't find nobody to let *him* live on credit. He had to pay cash. And if he had to chalk up many more accounts receivable he was going to borrow the schoolhouse blackboard. The Captain pointed out that if Bradley locked up his place, the boys would take it apart like a bear looking for grubs in a rotten stump, and if he tried to light out of town with his whiskey, they would track him down, and if they found him, he'd be living on considerable less than credit. You see, them punchers owed Bradley so much money they felt they had a kind of investment in the establishment, and wouldn't take kindly to his removing the chief article of trade.

Old Bradley got riled then. He said it was one hell of a pass, and what was the Captain there for? And what was the Judge there for? And the Captain asked Bradley what was *he* there for? He reminded Bradley how he had started giving credit so he would get all the business, and now he had got it, why, he should be satisfied. Yes, said Bradley, he was getting the business all right, and he had a pretty good notion who was giving it to him and in what location.

The Captain stayed cool as a cucumber while old Bradley was spitting and sputtering like a pump with a dried-out valve, and let on that this wasn't no big thing, just something that would all blow away before long. But every morning he sent me over to Bradley's doggery to count heads and see who was

9

just arrived and who had stayed on or left and what the mood was like. While I was there I picked up the Captain's meals for him, same as for the Judge, instead of having Bradley's Injun cook bring them over. That give me a chance to wait around a bit, which I done as best I could, like I done everything the Captain told me to do, ever since he was in charge of the company of cavalry there in Fort Besterman and I was riding point.

That was before he got the arrow in his hand and they had to cut it off because of the mortification, along with his arm, just above the elbow. He wasn't much good to the cavalry then, so he left them, and then they left *us*. You see, for quite a spell Fort Besterman hadn't been much more than a supply depot, being too far south to be bothered much by Red Cloud, and when the Government finally got a treaty out of the Oglala Sioux, Besterman didn't serve much purpose at all. So the Army asked the Captain wouldn't he stay there and look after things, and he said, "Winky, your time is just about up, isn't it?" So I stayed there with him. They call me Winky because I blink all the time ever since some of Red Cloud's braves got holt of me for a tolerable slow half-hour. It was my own damn fault, scouting too far ahead of the main troop, and when the Captain come up with the rest and drove the Injuns off he would of give me hell only he seen what they done and throwed up instead. He was younger then, and all the fighting he done was in the Rebellion, where people just shot one another or blew them up.

Well, it wasn't nice what the Injuns done to me, but at least they left me my hair, which is apt to get me into less trouble than the other. I told the Captain that—later, I mean—and he sort of laughed and then made me company clerk, seeing how painful it was for me to ride out for quite a spell afterwards. That was back in '67, and I stuck with him ever since, like a burr to a blanket. We was just the two of us after the Army left, and though we was supposed to keep an eye on things, there wasn't much to do except watch the prairie grass growing up on the parade ground. It was ghosty then, all them buildings silent and dark, but it wasn't ghosty long.

Pretty soon the people from the Hog Ranch begun moving in and taking over, which was a place close by on the other side of the river that had give the soldiers off duty something to do besides pester the Injun village down by the forks. The Hog Ranch was mostly ramshackly gin mills and a whorehouse, the kind of place that grew up wherever there was soldiers and pay day, with rusty tin cans and bottles all around and considerable human trash too. Most generally it would of been tore down or just left behind ten minutes after the troops pulled stakes. But the fort was right on the old Trail betwixt Douglas and Casper where the Chicago and Northwestern was supposed to be laying a spur up from the U.P. line, so the saloon-keepers and the whores decided to stick around for a while, scraping a living off the cowboys and whatever else blew their way, hoping for better times later on. They seen all them good Government-built warehouses and barracks standing empty and decided it was a sinful waste of taxpayers' money.

In less than a year the Hog Ranch had moved in, chandelier, tin cans, and all, and made theirselves right at home. The Captain wrote off to people who never answered, and then just let it slide. I said it was shameful to have such doings right there on a military post. He said there wasn't that much difference between the fort taking its dirty linen to the Hog Ranch and the Hog Ranch setting up its tubs in the fort. I said it wasn't Regulation. But the Captain held that the regulations had left with the soldiers, along with the uniforms and rifles. It was like a church, he said. When the congregation and the preacher moves out, it's just a place, same as any other.

"That might be so," I said. "But that's on account of the congregation not owning the church no more, while the Government still owns this fort. And so long as the Government owns it, ain't it right for the regulations to hold?"

"It's this way," said the Captain, patient as always. "The

Government owns this place, but it doesn't want it, while the Hog Ranch wants it, and thinks it has it, but it doesn't. The Government owns it, and should regulate it, but doesn't, and the people who live here can regulate it any way they want to, but there isn't any sanction from anybody or anything which gives them the right to regulate anything or anybody."

"But didn't the Army leave us in charge? Godalmighty, Captain, don't that mean something?"

"Yes, it means there are two of us, and thirty of them."

"But ain't we got the Government behind us?"

"About one hundred miles."

"Then you don't think they would back us up?"

"They might," he said, "if they got the message soon enough, providing we had the time to write it and the chance to mail it."

"Then what you're saying is that there ain't no authority in this goddam place besides you and me, which the Government pays but has otherwise forgot, and the Judge, which the Hog Ranch elected but without no legal right to do so. Otherwise there ain't nothing here by way of law and order."

"That's right," said the Captain. "So far as the U.S. Government and the Territory of Wyoming is concerned, this place is nowhere. Neutral ground."

"Yes," I said. "Until some wild bunch comes along and decides to take over. Then what?"

"That's about the size of it," he said.

When cows got to be big business so did Fort Besterman, and other folks begun to move in and run things, respectable people mostly, storekeepers and such, and next thing you know they had got a schoolhouse and a church built. They was forever holding town meetings, as they called them, and incorporating theirselves a dozen different ways, all in a great sweat over what was going to happen once the tracks come through. The place still didn't belong to nobody, but they went on acting as though it was theirs, and one of the biggest fights they had was what to *call* their goddam town.

A lot of the new people didn't much admire the old name, which the Army had borrowed off a colonel who didn't need it any more on account of being teased out into the hills one day by Spotted Tail, far enough out so the Injuns could take their time massacring him and a hundred others, not counting horses, mules, and a dog. The new people didn't like calling their town after a soldier who got whipped by Injuns, and they also thought "Besterman" had a sort of Hebrew ring to it and just didn't have the right Western sound. So they finally voted to call the place Invincible, which was a name full of the progressive spirit and guts, they thought, and would help trade once the rail line come through. They painted two signs:

INVINCIBLE

and stuck them on either side of town. But a cowpuncher with a can of paint come along, and then the signs read

INVISIBLE

only pretty soon they was so full of .45-caliber holes you couldn't of told what they said if you had wanted to. Most everybody went right on calling the place Besterman except for them who kept calling it the Hog Ranch.

The Captain said he thought they ought to name their town after the Judge, seeing how he had been there longer than anybody else, having been the oldest-living and the longest-living member of the Hog Ranch, and having carried the credit with him when he moved up to the fort along with the rest. The Captain said without the Judge and the jail and the rooms upstairs where he lived and done his presiding there wouldn't be no town to hang a name on, that it would of dried up and blowed away long ago. He claimed that if the Judge ever died, whatever stage manager had set up that town would most likely come back to take it down and put it on a wagon and drive on farther west with it.

The Captain was always saying things like that, or quoting poetry at me. The poetry was the worst part. I'd rather be cussed at and damned for a fool any time. When a man cusses at you, you got a choice, but when a man quotes poetry at you,

13

all you can do is stand there and look like a sick jackass till it's over and you can crawl away.

Well, no doubt about it, the Judge was the nail that held that town in place. He wasn't a real judge, with a law degree and cowhide-covered books and all, but from early on people had got in the habit of coming to him for a judgment betwixt theirselves. I don't rightly know why, unless it was because he wore that plug hat he had picked up somewheres along the way, an old bunged-in beaver with holes where a bullet had gone through. When he stood just so, you could spot through them holes straight as any transit. Or maybe it was because he was always sober, no matter how much Red Eye he had drunk, and they could always count on him being upright when every other man in town was on his back, or inclining in that direction. Anyways, when the Hog Ranch got big enough to need a law man to keep the cowboys and soldiers from killing each other when both was in town and whores was in short supply, they held a meeting and made him a justice of the peace, and then went to work and built him a little log jailhouse. He lived in one side and gave judgments, and whoever happened to be tearing up the ranch the night before lived in the other side.

When the Hog Ranch moved itself up to the fort, they give the Judge Post Headquarters, which was the finest building there, with lots of room and even a four-cell lockup in back, with regular iron furniture made in Pittsburgh, Pennsylvania. But he didn't like where it was located, which was right in the center of the fort. He said there wasn't no view from there, or at least none that he wanted to see. So the people tore it all down and moved it to where the Judge thought it should be, at the east end of town, so he could get a good view of the road where it come in off the flats, right up to where it become the main street.

They had tore down the stockade early on, but the Judge had them build his place two stories high anyhow, to make sure there wasn't nothing betwixt him and the road. The Post HQ had been only one story, so the new building ended up toler-able narrow, with an office and the lockup downstairs and the Judge's room and the room where he done his presiding up-stairs, but he liked it fine. From his window he could see all he wanted to of the road, and whatever else there was off to the east he was of a mind to look at. But it did seem like he was mostly interested in the farthest point on that road which the eye could see, and didn't give much of a damn about the count-less other interesting sights closer in to town, like the grave-yard and Anse Pulcherd, a feeble-minded feller who used to take his clothes off and stray out of town till somebody thought to fetch him back.

Well, nobody put up no more buildings on the Judge's side of the street, out of respect for him, but a couple others went up on the other side, including Bradley's doggery. Bradley clapped it together out of salvage from the Army stables about a hundred feet farther east than anybody else. He did that so he could call his place the "First Chance Saloon," and he reckoned on getting a little extra business that way, along with selling on credit. He figured everybody else was too lazy to put up an-other saloon farther on out, there still being a couple unused Government buildings left, and he was right, too, for all the good it done him. Like the Judge, he built hisself two stories, and he lived upstairs in front with that darling wife of his and rented out four square holes in back he called rooms to any-body hard up enough to believe him.

When I got down to Bradley's that morning the gang had already gone inside and there was only these two new fellers rubbing theirselves and stretching, like they had just got done riding a considerable ways. They was all coated over with red muck from the middle down, and I guessed they had crawled up onto the boardwalk from the street, which was more like a riverbed where the river has just changed its mind and gone another way. There was boards strung across it, here and there, so you could get from one side to the other, and it wasn't safe to try to navigate it any other way. Somebody told me just a week earlier that a keg of nails had broke loose in front of Lafe Chancellor's store and rolled off the boardwalk into the muck. Lafe had prodded around with a pole for half a hour but he never did sound that keg, and afterwards people was a little more respectful when they crossed them planks.

Then I see the two mules tethered there, up to their knees in the stuff and slathered saddle-high, and I figured that Besterman had just took on a couple more deficits. I give them newcomers a squint in passing, but there was so much misty steam there in front of Bradley's on account of the horseshit and such which had got mixed in with the muck that it was hard to make them out. I see they was dressed in overalls and sheepskin jackets like everybody else and was wearing floppy old felt hats that had been drunk out of and slept in and used to fan fires with, regulation wear for them days. Then I looked back at the mules and seen for the first time they *was* mules, and that sort of stopped me. "Mules?" I remember thinking. "There ain't a self-respecting cowpuncher in the Territory rides a *mule*."

But it was just half a thought, as you might say, and I was almost past them and into the doggery when they begun waving their fingers at each other. They went at it strong with this semaphore of theirs, and the one facing me, a young kid, palish and with blue eyes, was working both jaws at the same time, only without no sound coming out. Now I had seen that same kind of thing before, back in K.C., and right away I knew what it was. Not Injun signs, you see, but deaf and dumb. They was mutes, or at least one of them was.

It ain't polite to stare, and I was afraid Blue Eyes would look my way sooner or later, so I started into Bradley's like before, when the other one, the big feller with his back to me, he took off his hat to scratch around for a thought and that was it for me. I about-faced and quick-marched back down the boardwalk, knowing the Captain would want to hear about *this* one, and before breakfast, too. In them days, before he got married and regularly settled in, the Captain used to bed down in the jailhouse, right there in the office underneath the Judge. He had an Army cot, along with a table and a chest of drawers, and a couple splint-bottom chairs. There was a stove, too, and a washstand, with a regular pitcher, basin, and thundermug below, hand-painted and left behind with the Captain by Mrs. Molly Finch, who was the Major's wife, when she left with all the others. Not very fancy, but all right after barracks living.

I could hear the leathers on the cot squeak when I knocked on the door, and then the Captain said, "That you, Winky?"

"Yes, sir, it is, Captain."

Then there was a little quiet while he looked at his clock to see why the alarm hadn't gone off, and saw I was early getting there, which I seldom was.

"Something wrong?"

"Well," I said, "I got some news from down at Bradley's that'll interest you, maybe."

I could hear him getting up, and I knew he was setting on the edge of his cot so as to collect his thoughts and count his molars.

"You got my breakfast out there?"

"No, sir, Captain, I don't. I sort of figured you'd want this piece of news before you ate."

"Well, well," he said, and I could hear him getting up and sliding into his britches. Then, clump, clump, into his boots. "What's that, Winky?"

"Couple new fellers just arrived," I said, giving it to him slow, which is the way to do with bad news, especially when the man you are giving it to ain't but half awake yet.

"Is that what you wanted to tell me?" he said, in that dry way of his, so I reckoned I was giving it out a trifle too slow.

"Aw, no," I said. "These fellers is *different*."

"You mean they've got money?" he said. "Or jobs to hand out?" I could hear him fussing with the stove in there, rattling the grate and the lid and pouring in coal oil. You could smell it clear through the door. "We could use a little of that kind of difference."

"One's a nigger, Captain."

He was quiet for a bit, not a long bit, and if you hadn't of knowed him as well as I did, you wouldn't even of noticed that bit or thought nothing of it. Then he begun to whistle

you know, keeping his own time by thunking the poker into the firewood. He was always one for fussing with a new fire.

"Where are they?" he said.

"Why, over at Bradley's, like everybody else. Outside, anyways. Or leastwise that's where I left them two minutes ago." I waited, but he didn't say nothing more, so I asked him if he wanted me to go back over and get his breakfast.

"Come on in, Winky," he said. "Let me give you a cup of coffee." That was his way, every time. It would work up to where I was just about to set out to do something we both knew ought to be done, something we'd been talking about for maybe five or ten minutes, and *then* he'd ask me in for a cup of coffee or some other little thing which would take up ten minutes more. It was the way he was.

Well, I went in, and there he was standing over the stove, whistling

and whacking away at the fire with his one good arm, the other held tight to his side in that pinned-up sleeve. If you've ever noticed, there's some one-armed men that'll waggle their stump every now and then, as if they had forgot it wasn't a regular arm no more, but the Captain never did. He'd use it to hold something, like a bottle he was opening, but the rest of the time he kept it standing at attention, so to speak, straight up and down.

"Captain," I said. "You're beating that poor fire to death, again."

"It's the wood," he said. "You've been bringing me wet wood . . . *again.*"

"If I have," I said, "it's only because there ain't no other kind."

He didn't say nothing to this, and never did, but just kept beating away and beating away until I couldn't stand it no more. "Let me try her," I said, like always, and like always he handed me the poker.

Well, I didn't want it, so I put it down. Then I took the coal oil and some dry twigs we used for kindling, and I opened the grate and shoved the brush in under the splitlings, and poured some of that sweet-smelling coal oil over it all. There was still life in the embers so she popped up right away without no match, and I fanned away with my old Army tile till she was burning nice. It don't do to mess around with a new fire. It discourages her, knocks the life out of her. All a fire needs is kindness and a little air. And coal oil when the wood is wet.

The Captain washed out his coffeepot with a dipper of water from the bucket slung by his washstand, and after he had dumped it out the window he put in two more dippers of water and set it down on the stove to heat. Then he sat on the bed and pointed to one of the splint-bottoms, which I climbed onto backwards so as to straddle it and have a place to rest my arms. It was right cozy in there, with the new fire crackling away, and somehow things didn't seem in such a hurry as before.

"Well, what's he look like, Winky?"

"Jesus, I don't know, Captain. All I seen was the back of his head."

"Was he big? Small? Young? Old?"

"Oh, he's *big*, Captain," I said. "Real big. I don't know how old he is, but he ain't *old*, if you know what I mean. There ain't no cotton in his wool, and he stands like he was made to pick high apples."

"You said there was two of them."

"The other's white, and on the skimpy side. Young, too— just a kid, really. Got china-blue eyes. And he's pale, like maybe he was sick a while ago but has got some color back."

All the time we was talking I was trying to remember what else there was about them, and then it come to me so quick I almost couldn't get the words out. It was just like a crowd trying to leave a place when a fight starts outside and they want to get there before it's over, everybody jammed up at the door and starting a few fights of their own. But the Captain got the general idea.

"*Both* of them?"

"Well, I can't say for sure. The boy, he was facing me, and I could see his mouth working, like they do sometimes, but both of them was waggling away like crazy. Still, if I had to choose which one, I'd say the boy. There's something mighty peculiar about him, anyway. And who ever heard of a deaf-and-dumb nigger?"

"Is Fiddler Jones still in town?"

"Old Yaller Eyes? I reckon he is. He was here until last night, leastwise. Up to closing time, I mean. I don't know where he sleeps, though, if he *does* sleep."

Now Fiddler Jones was from Texas, and was in the way of being the orneriest man in the Territory. Before he come our way he had been run out of every town he'd been in, and if he had stayed with us a whole week, we'd of found reasons to run him out ourselves. He was a regular devil and looked the part, a tall, long-nosed, dark feller, with black hair standing on end all over his head. Outrageous hair it was, and I swear he wore it that way on purpose. He kept it crammed under a greasy old sombrero most of the time, and that hat was a miracle, too. Whoever erected that holy wonder must of used Pike's Peak for a block, because it was the biggest goddam cone you ever see, with a brim to match, held up by somebody's hatpin the size of a skewer, with a pearl on one end big as a pigeon's egg. Jones had got the sombrero off a dead greaser, he said, and all around it where the band should be he had a chain of holy medals took off other greasers as well, and they was loose and jangled when he walked, like his spurs, only softer, which was also Mexican.

Well, that hat was a regular entertainment, spotted and stained all over like an Injun pony and so dented and full of holes it looked like a cheese grater somebody had tossed in front of a stampede. But when Jones wanted a real effect, a twenty-dollar effect, he would take the sombrero off and turn his hair loose. It was for all the world like the spines on a worried porcupine, springing out in all directions. You had to take a step or two backwards when it happened. You just had to.

Jones had dirty yaller eyes, like hunks of amber with bits of stuff in them, and they glowed like amber too. He must of had some coyote in him, I reckon, to get hatched with eyes like that. He was fond of aiming them eyes at you while he was talking, and all the time he would be smiling and smiling—he had yaller teeth, too—only it wasn't really no smile. And his voice was raspy, not loud, but a steady rasp like a sockful of gravel being rubbed slow between your hands. He had a joky way about him, if a trifle on the mean side, and he could tell stories like no other man. I've heard about him getting one poor bastard laughing that he had a gun on, and when the sucker was laughing so hard he couldn't stop, with tears running his face, and holding onto his wagon to keep from collapsing into a pile of mush, it was then Jones shot him—bing, right in the forehead, which was his favorite target.

But maybe the gaudiest thing about Jones was his vest. It was made out of silk, and was yaller too, and dirty, same as his eyes and teeth. When you first seen him, that was what you noticed, his vest and his eyes, because the rest of him was so dark. Then he would smile, if you want to call it that, and put those teeth on display, and while you was staring at them cubes, yaller as a row of old dice, his hand would catch your eye as it went up towards his sombrero, which you hadn't noticed before, and as soon as you did he would yank it off, leaving you so upset and nervous you would forget everything but his hair for a minute, and next his eyes would get to you again, staring at you like the glass ones they use when they stuff a dead animal for the man who shot him, and then the vest and next the teeth again. It was the damnedest thing.

Where Jones was and there were other men, he was always at the center of attention, but there was always a little space around him, not much, maybe only two or three feet, because there was something about him kept you at a distance, and I don't mean his smell, neither, though that helped. Nor was it his easy way with a gun, nor his sombrero, nor his eyes, nor his teeth, nor his vest, nor his hair. Maybe it was all of it together, which was mighty damn scary, or maybe it was something else. All I know is that Jones wasn't what you'd call a big man, being tall and lanky, but when he come into a room, the *effect* was big. Like a wolverine, which the Injuns call carcajou and move out of any place he moves into. Because wherever Jones was, he was the resident devil, as you might say, and nobody else cared to apply for the job.

I've known considerable many bad men in my day, but there was only one that didn't have at least one feller who could call him "pard," and throw his arm around his shoulder or pat him on the back or touch him in some harmless way or other and call him an old son-of-a-bitch, and that was Fiddler Jones. But men would always gather where he was, and listen and laugh at his jokes, jus' 's though he wasn't a bad man and a mean one to boot. Maybe the reason they crowded around him all the time was they was afraid to be there alone.

He was born plain C. A. Jones, standing for Cussed Awful, I guess, but somewhere back along that road leading out of Texas he had picked up a piece of lead in his shoulder that was meant for a place farther south, and the lead had stayed there for good, giving him a new name on top of the bad one he already had. You see, the bullet was in his left shoulder, and it bothered him some in cool weather, so he got in the habit of rubbing it with his gun barrel when it was hot, absent-minded like, because the heat felt so good on the scar. It didn't matter whether he was shooting tin cans or a drunk Injun, as soon as he was done firing, up would come that old Colt .45 and saw back and forth over his shoulder. Jones always lowered his face in that direction, and it was for all the world like he had a goddam fiddle there, and that's where his nickname come from, along with the piece of lead, from Texas.

"He done anything we could use to run him out of town or lock him up until that pair has moved on?"

"Well, over in Casper . . ."

"That won't do. It's got to be *here.*"

"Captain, we could run him out on general principles. Everybody knows . . ."

"That won't do either. But it's hard for me to believe that Jones has been here two whole days without committing some kind of mayhem."

Well, that was true enough, but I hadn't heard of anything he had done since arriving, and when Fiddler Jones done something, why you always heard about it, because it was always so outrageous, like the rest of him. Take the time he painted that schoolma'am's behind, over in Casper. He was just passing by the schoolhouse and seen the paintbucket the feller had left there, with the brush laying across the stir-stick, so he picked up the brush, got it full of red paint, stepped into the room where the teacher was writing on the board, hoisted up her skirts, ran down her bloomers, and painted her ass bright red, all so quick that they say her chalk never left the board. Then he carried her outside, throwed a half-hitch round her ankle and run her up the pole in place of the flag. News like that gets around. It was a shameful thing to do, and there was considerable talk around Casper about hunting Jones down and having a little stake-out on top of an ant hill, womanhood being sacred to the Code of the West and all, but nothing ever come of it, and seldom did when Fiddler Jones was involved.

"Maybe by tonight . . ." I said.

"Yes," said the Captain, "I'm sure of that, and it's just what I don't want. Why in hell did Jones and that black man have to show up here at the same time? Those are the kind of odds that would break a gambler's heart. Why, there couldn't be more than a dozen black men in the whole Territory, to say nothing of the great wide West, and half of them are extinct. And if there's more than *one* Fiddler Jones this side of St. Louis, God help the country."

Well, the water was boiling by then, so the Captain got up and tossed in a handful of coffee and chicory, along with some scraps of eggshell he always had Bradley send over with his breakfast eggs, and then he come back to the cot and sat down again. There was his coat hanging on a peg overhead and he reached up and took out his pipe and pouch.

"Want some?" he says, like always, and like always I said, "No, sir, but I'll chew if you don't mind," which he never did. He had a spittoon in there just for me to use, because he didn't chew at all, no more than I smoked.

He lit up and I bit off, and we both sat there saying nothing for a while, waiting for the coffee. He didn't say nothing because he was thinking, and I didn't because I *couldn't*. So soon as I had that chaw down to size I said, "You want me to tell the Judge?"

"What, and get him all upset? I guess not."

"Then it ain't his nigger, you don't think?"

"If it was a man of seventy or upwards, it might be. If it was a black man that old, I'd say it was about as likely his as finding jobs tomorrow for all the cow tramps in the Territory."

"Well, he isn't," I said. "Couldn't of been more than thirty."

"Then that increases the odds considerably. I doubt if even old Barnes would take odds like those."

I had to laugh at that one, and got a bit of juice in my beard because of it. "Shit," I said, "old Barnes will bet on snow in August if you'll only take his marker."

"Well," he said, "if you want to add to your collection of Barnes's markers, you just get him to bet this is the Judge's long-lost friend. Because it isn't, and between you and me, Winky, it isn't ever going to be."

Well, it wasn't the first time the Captain had said that, but it always made me nervous, and I said, "You ain't ever told *him* that, have you, Captain?"

"No, and I have never told a child there is no Santa Claus, either. Why should I? He knows it himself, but he'd never believe it if I or you or anybody told him. There's a part of him sits up there arguing with the other part, but the other part wins out every time. I doubt if the believing part of him even *listens* to the thinking part any more. It's like a man with a nagging wife. She pesters him for the first thirty years, and for the next thirty he doesn't pay any more attention to her than to the squeaky board in the porch steps she's been after him to fix all those years. The Judge *believes* in his black man, and there isn't an argument invented that can convince him he's wrong. He accepts it on faith, like you accept your shadow at high noon. It's his religion, Winky."

"Yes, sir," I said, letting one go into the spittoon. "I reckon it is, and I expect he's up there right now taking communion."

The Captain filled two tin cups with coffee, keeping the grounds back with an old, chewed-up spoon. Then he took his bottle of Red Eye under his stump and twisted out the cork so as to season the coffee and help it along. He handed me one cup

25

and then hoisted his own upwards. "Here's to him," he said.

Well, I give him "Judge," but before I could drink any of that coffee I had to take my quid out, which was a shame because it was hardly worked at all. It was always that way with the Captain, giving me coffee after I had just bit off a chaw. A pipe-smoking man and a chewing man live different lives, there ain't no two ways about it.

II

When I got back over to Bradley's the nigger was still out on the boardwalk, only now he was sitting down, with his back against the wall. Whether it was the ride or the view or what, I don't know, but he didn't seem to have much starch in him. He was more or less folded once over, like wet overalls hanging on a line. Inside, the kid was standing at the bar talking to Bradley, the only one up there. The rest was all sitting around on the benches set up near Bradley's big pot-belly stove, smoking and drinking whatever they had got out of him that morning—mostly beer it looked like. There was a number who was just smoking, and had got a respectable cloud raised around them, and judging from the stink, there was considerable cabbage and such shit mixed in with the rest.

Bradley had only just got the fire going, so it was cold in there, and most everybody had on their coat and hat, so along with the smoke there was a good deal of steam rising up around the stove from all the damp clothes. When the wind carried the cloud in your direction you wasn't sure whether you was in a stable or a meatpacker's or a burning dump. Sitting there with all the rest was the young gambler they had throwed off the Douglas stage a couple days earlier. He didn't have on much covering, and had worked himself so close to the stove he had to keep turning around so as not to catch one side on fire, and he kept his hands tucked in out of sight for once, instead of eternally shuffling cards. But his jaw was working, same as ever, for he was an interesting feller, full of wild tales about his travels, which was mostly done on the end of a blind baggage or on the rods underneath. He held that America was full of opportunities if a man only knew them when he seen them, and that the freight train was the poor man's Pullman. The U.P., he said, stood for Universal Promise, and it was his opinion that Huntington and Crocker and the rest of that pack was the world's greatest philanthropists. He said they had made it possible for anybody who wanted to to go out and share in the opportunities of the West. They was his model, every time. His name was Something Sturgis, or Sturgis Something, but we got to calling him Leland Stanford for sport. He didn't seem to mind it at all.

The kid was bareheaded now, long, lanky blond hair hanging straight down almost to the shoulders, same as Custer done, and kept flicking it back while talking in a low voice to old Bradley, nervous and quavery. Bradley had his head down and was wiping at a glass, wiping and wiping and growling back or saying nothing. I went on past, back to where his Injun cook was kept in a little galley-like place with a stove and pots and pans. She was just up, and sitting on the edge of her cot, weaving her hair into braids, though how she done it without a steel fid was a wonder. I give her the order, and seeing how her fire wasn't yet lit and most likely she would have to hunt the Captain's eggs up where she kept a couple hens under the doggery, I dug out my quid and went back out to the bar to enjoy it and admire myself in the big mirror over the bottles in back.

Even though I was standing down at the far end of the bar, I could hear everything the kid and Bradley was saying. Sound travels in cold air, you know, and the wind blowing along the bar helped considerable. If it had been only a few degrees colder in there, I could of broke the words off and taken them back for the Captain to thaw out and listen to for hisself.

Well, the kid was doing most of the talking. Old Bradley had took a good holt on that glass, which had a bottom to it as thick as a bull's-eye in a lantern, and was polishing away like it was his last, shaking his head and saying he didn't keep no rooms for no damned niggers, and that his other rooms was all filled up. The kid kept going on and on, in a weak, shaky voice, about how they had been riding for two days, and if they didn't lie down they was going to fall down, and they didn't care what kind of bed it was, or who they had to share it with, Injun or bedbug, so long as it was thicker than a piece of paper and softer than a board. And Bradley said he *reckoned* they didn't care who they slept with, the kid leastwise, seeing what was out on the porch, but the kid didn't bat an eye, just kept talking in that funny voice, saying how tired they was, and they would sleep in the stable or the hencoop or even the pig-pen, so long as there was room to stretch out. But Bradley kept shaking his head No, No, No, and allowed as if he had too much respect for his hogs even if there was room, if he kept any hogs, which he didn't, unless you counted that room full of punchers.

I begun to wonder why the kid was so damned het up about staying at Bradley's. There was a couple other places in town, stables and the like, where they and the mules could of got took care of. But the kid come to that, and without no help from me. You see, that nigger was good medicine, according to the kid. He was deaf and dumb, maybe, but he had powers nobody else had. It was he who picked out Bradley's and said they should stay there, and the kid was bound and possessed they *would* stay there, cost being no object. That nigger's powers had always done good by them before, in all sorts of cases, and everybody always come out ahead by doing what those powers told them to do. But old Bradley said there was only one power a goddam nigger had, and that was a skull you could crack green hazelnuts on.

"Well, now, Mr. Bradley, I'd add another to that. It seems to me you've missed one of the nigra's prime attributes. Why, I recollect seeing a boy somethin' shorter than the one you've got on display out front that had a pecker stickin' out most as far as the branch he was a-hangin' from."

There it was, that damned pebbly voice, and I didn't have to look towards the door to know there was a yaller vest and yaller eyes at the other end of the bar. That was Jones's way, every time, to come sliding up so he could catch you by surprise. It wasn't that he come sifting in. Hell, no. There wasn't nothing sneaky about Fiddler Jones. It was just that he had a way of getting into a place without nobody seeing him, and then more or less spreading himself so that everybody seen him at once.

"Yes, sir," Jones said, "and I thought to myself, 'Now there's a thing worth having,' so I took it along with me. It dried out right handsome, and I used it for a quirt until I give it to a Mexican gal who had took a fancy to it when I told her the story."

Well, Bradley kept quiet. He looked up, but only because he was a mite surprised, along with the rest of us, and then looked right back at his glass when he seen who it was. You wouldn't of hardly known that Jones was one of his best customers. Considering the short time he had been in town, Fiddler had chalked up considerable credit on the slate, only he didn't call it credit. He called it insurance.

"That a glass or a telescope lens you're polishing at, Mr. Bradley?"

"A glass," said Bradley, still not looking up and not very brash, neither, which he had been with the kid.

"Then I guess it's clean enough," said Jones, taking something out of his vest pocket and sort of slapping it down on the mahogany—only it was pine brown-stained. "Whyn't you fill it up for me."

If Bradley had been surprised before, he was downright amazed this time. "Where'd you get *that?*" he asked, picking up the yaller boy and holding it up to the light so as to look at it.

"Found her in the street," said Jones. "I don't like to keep gold idle, it ain't patriotic, so I thought I'd invest in some of your good whiskey."

"Bottle or a barrel?"

"Just that clean glass full," says Jones. "And while you're at it, fill up a dozen more for the boys."

He raised his voice for this last one, and the bar lined up so fast it was like it had growed a whole row of smiles at the sight of that open bottle. They was all aimed at Jones, except for the kid, who was looking down at two empty hands. Bradley come along, filling glasses as he went, and he passed right by the kid without stopping.

"Hold it," said Jones. He had helped himself to a can of deviled ham which he was opening with his clasp knife, but he seen the pass-by just the same. "You missed one."

"He tried to come in here with that damned nigger."

Jones sniffed, and I seen his eyes tighten, but he give a broad smile as if his daddy had been an Abolitionist. "It's a free country, Mr. Bradley," he said, scooping out the ham with his fingers. "He's got as much right to try and bring that nigger in here as you have to throw him out." Jones got all the meat from that can wrapped around two fingers and then stuck the fingers into his mouth and pulled them out clean. "Serve um!" he said, somehow getting his words past the meat though they did come out sort of mushy.

Bradley filled my glass, which was the last one, and set the bottle on the bar. "He wants me to find a bed for his goddam nigger, too," he said.

"Mr. Bradley," said Jones, "I don't give a shit what he wants of you. I don't care if he wants his damn nigger to sleep with that buckskin bitch you call a wife. Shut your head and pour the kid some whiskey."

Now it just wouldn't do to get Fiddler Jones upset, so Bradley give a little whine and started back with his bottle. But the kid looked up at Jones and said, "I'm much obliged, but I can buy my own whiskey," polite and nice as a Sunday-school teacher.

Well, them yaller eyes was a study. Jones looked like a hound pup that has just discovered a porcupine ain't a rabbit. Some of the smiles at that bar turned to other things, and begun to fade back toward the benches. But old Jones was calm, very calm. There was more twists and turns to that bastard than there is in the whole length of the Powder River. You just never knew what was ahead, around the next bend, so to speak. He just cleared his throat, took a sip of his whiskey, and said, "Oh, now, boy, I didn't mean that you *could*n't. I just meant you should be included in the general treat."

The kid looked down some more, and then back up at Jones, and then at Bradley, and finally back to Jones. It was quite a journey, and I was plumb wore out at the end of it.

"That's very kind of you," the kid said at last. "I accept."

So the kid got a drink, and then Jones got his toast. "Here's to Blondie," he said, and hoisted his glass to the company assembled. "Everybody drink or die." And they did. Even Bradley. That was the second time that day I had to take out that damned quid, and I was so disgusted I throwed it away.

Well, Fiddler next give the Governor's health, then the President's, and it wasn't long before that gold eagle was spreading its wings inside everybody, including the little gambler, who got taken in on the third round. Bradley started snatching empty glasses out of people's hands before the spirit of good cheer worked itself up to talking about more credit, but then Blondie piped up, pulling a little sack out from under somewhere: "Drinks for everybody once around."

You never seen a hog change spots so like that Bradley. He smiled on that kid like the prodigal child returned and snatched up the little shammy bag like an express train picking up the mail. He emptied it on his scales, totaled it, and then come tearing around with the bottle in less time than Fiddler took to clean out his second can of tomatoes. It did look like the kid had found a way to Bradley's heart, and I guessed they wouldn't have too much trouble finding something to sleep on when they wanted it.

The Injun come out just then with the basket of grub, and so I had to leave. I asked Bradley to keep a little of the kid's whiskey for me, but he was too busy to listen, and everybody was whooping and hollering, so I didn't push myself, but left with the basket. It did seem as though the day was starting out right at Bradley's, and I told the Captain so when I give him his breakfast.

He sat there staring down at his plate, which had that wild look fried eggs can give it. Maybe they reminded him of Fiddler Jones. Finally he sliced his fork through one of them and begun to eat away, sopping up the yolk with a piece of the Injun's corn bread.

"Just one big happy family over there," he says. "Shows you what religion will do, because if this town has a religion, it's 'drinks for the crowd.' "

Well, he didn't say nothing more, so I reckoned he wanted to be left alone with his eggs. I started out for the Judge's room, though there wasn't no hurry, because it was only cold corn dodgers and buttermilk, like always, but then the Captain looks up and says, "Don't say anything to the Judge, Winky."

"Hmph!" I said. "Didn't you tell me that already? Until I hear different, I ain't doing different."

"Fine," he said. "No sense in getting him all upset. He's been in pretty good shape lately, and I'd like to keep him that way."

"I ain't saying nothing until the orders is changed."

"Come on back down for another cup of coffee when you're done up there."

"Maybe I ought to get on over to Bradley's right off, and keep an eye on things."

"You stop by here, first. Bradley's whiskey will hold out for a while yet."

I went on up to the Judge's room, and there he was, like always, keeping watch on the road into town. "Morning, Judge," I said.

He swung around in his old chair and give me that funny look of his which was like the looks people give you if you wake them up and they don't exactly know where they are. He had queer eyes, anyway, blue and flat, the color of carpenter's chalk. They was smallish and set way back in that little face of his, which was all squinched in the middle of his head. It was a regular baby face, and he had a baby's head, too, round and bald. Where his hair had been there was a sort of purplish blaze, on account of a Injun had tore off his scalp, being so eager to get it he didn't stop to make sure he had earned it. When the Judge went out of doors or into his courtroom he kept it covered with his old plug hat, but up in that room he went bald. And a colorful sight he was, too, like unto a baboon's ass.

All day long he kept company up there with a whiskey jug, working at it so slow you could hardly tell except for the smell, which cut through the old socks and bedclothes and seegar smoke. His face showed it, though, because it got redder and redder during the day, and that scar got gaudier and gaudier. By the end of the day he was a regular decoration, and it was almost as though he was the one that lit up the eastern hills. He sort of looked like the sun, anyway, the kind you see in pictures with a little face drawed on it.

Well, he sat at his window from dawn to dusk, and sometimes he slept there, settling down in his chair as soon as it was dark. When light come, his eyes opened up and he went right on watching. He was a rooster for waking up with the dawn. He sat there in the window like some dog that's lost its owner, waiting on the same street corner week after week, looking into a thousand faces every day. Maybe the man's dead, or in jail, but he sits there anyhow, waiting and waiting. Maybe he's forgot what the man looks like, or maybe what he's waiting for, but it don't make no difference.

From his window he could see the road, like I said, and the river, too, which run off towards the southeast, a kind of easy scrawl of cottonwoods and willows, wandering this way and that. The road come in along the river there, only it run straight as a carpenter's rule, and at that time of year was a red line across the sage and greasewood, like the first slash a trapper makes when he starts to skin something he just killed. That road went on, through the town and towards Idaho, but the Judge didn't seem to care none where it went, just where it come from, out of the east. The Captain used to say the only west that road had for the Judge was in his eyes, where it was reflected back, you see, and that everybody who might come into town rode up that red line right into his head. They might ride on to California, but the only west they had so far as the Judge was concerned was what lay behind his eyes, and that was a Territory no man could come to the end of.

Well, when he turned around and looked at me I could see his eyes was still full of the road, as flat and blue as the sky above it. I put the basket down and took the things out for him, along with the cup of coffee I had brung up from downstairs. There was a little table by the Judge's chair that he ate off of when he was of a mind to eat and which the flies ate off of all the time. There was always flies in his room, on account of he kept his windows shut, from May to October, buzzing and bumping around the walls and the ceiling and speckling the window glass. The Judge didn't mind them none that I could ever tell. A fly could light on his head, take a stroll down his nose, and sit there cleaning his wings, and the Judge wouldn't ever move. Oh, maybe he'd twitch his nose or a patch of skin on his cheek once and a while, like a cow does, but I never seen him swat one ever.

The Judge hadn't always been like that, of course. When he first moved up to the fort he spent a good deal of time strolling around town like everybody else, or sitting in a chair in front of the jailhouse, watching the goings-on and waving and talking to the people passing by. He had a high-pitched voice, kind of like a boy's, and he usually spoke nearly in a whisper so you couldn't tell. If a man wouldn't come up to him to hear what he had to say, he would lift hisself up out of the chair and amble over to him to say it. He was very passel-gutted, even in them days, with thinnish arms and legs. His stomach hung down like a sack of wet meal, and when he walked it was like a pregnant woman, slow and careful. He wasn't a strong man, but there was something about him that got respect. Nobody ever hit him or shot at him, and if that plug hat of his ever got knocked off I never heard of it.

In those days, even, he kept his eyes on the road into town. At first the Captain and me thought it was part of his job as he seen it, along with the old horse pistol, a Navy Colt it was, he wore strapped over his frock coat and jeans, and that tin badge somebody had pinned on him for a joke but which he wore till it become the real thing. But then we saw he was always looking down the road, where it come into town from the east, and never the other way, and we figured it was a personal matter, and hadn't nothing to do with his job, trouble being as likely to come from the one direction as the other. It was plain he was watching for somebody in particular who would be coming from the east, and he didn't seem nervous or afraid, so it wasn't somebody that was after him, but more likely somebody he was looking forward to seeing again, whoever it was. As time passed he took to staying in his chair more and more, keeping it turned so he could look down the main street towards the east. In the winter he kept to his bedroom window except when he was presiding, and then one spring he just didn't come down.

By that time the Captain had took over most of his law-keeping duties, so it didn't make much difference, and when it come to presiding, the Judge was his old self, good as always. People would come up before him with a fight so tangled up you thought the only thing they could do was toss it out and start a new one. And he would sit there with the flies crawling over his face and listen and listen, half asleep it seemed like, and then when they was done he would sit there a while longer, and then he'd start to talk in that little voice of his and when he got done it was all settled. People might go away unhappy or even mad, but there wasn't nobody went away dissatisfied. He was a natural-born judge, there wasn't no getting around it, a regular Solomon, and yet he didn't have no books but a Bible, which he only used to give oaths on. It was all wore on the outside, but inside it was clean and white. I once saw him read a newspaper, and it took him three days to get through it.

The Captain said the reason he was a good judge even though he was touched in the head was that he judged with his heart, and so long as the two kept their distance, he could go on judging forever, looking at things clear and deep, taking them like they was, not like he thought they should be. That's why he didn't need any law books. From time to time a lawyer would show up in town, the way they always done, hoping to work up a little business off the range feuds, but they riled the Judge with the big words they used, and people caught on quick and left off giving them their custom.

The Judge liked things simple, and he took his breakfast that way, too, corn dodgers and buttermilk, every day. For supper he always had fried pork and cabbage, or maybe greens when we could get them, and beans when there wasn't nothing else. Sometimes he would take a fresh slab of beef for a change, but he favored the other, and always acted like it was a feast, like he hadn't ate that sort of truck for an age, sitting there looking out his window even while he was eating, so that considerable slipped out and run down his shirt and vest.

I went back down to the Captain's room, and he had done

eating and was sitting back on the bunk, smoking his pipe. It was that cavalry pipe of his, about two inches long, the kind you can keep in your jaws while you're riding along at a gallop. Out of habit he always took that one up when he was planning a campaign, so I guessed the goings-on in the doggery was on his mind, and it was.

"Any idea where he got that gold?"

"He said he found it in the street," I said. "But he must of dredged for it, or sluiced it out. I imagine you could find interesting things out there if you went deep enough, say ten or twelve feet. You heard about Lafe Chancellor's keg . . . ?"

"I mean the boy. I wouldn't begin to wonder where Jones found that golden eagle. I wouldn't dare."

"He never said," I told him. "He just pulled it out and plopped it down. Must of been two ounces in that little sack. How much whiskey you reckon that'll buy?"

The Captain prodded into his pipe with the end of a matchstick. He fussed with his tobacco about as much as he done with his fires, and got about the same results, too.

"I guess Bradley'll stop his bitching for a while. Unless they decide to tear down his doggery by way of celebration, now that the drought is over."

"Think I ought to get on over there, Captain?"

He didn't say nothing, just set to puffing away at his pipe, so I got a cup of coffee and considerable grounds and sat back down on the splint-bottom chair to wait for orders, because I knew he was planning his campaign. When we used to go out with the troop, he would always get his charts packed away so he could pull them out, one, two, three, according to the country we was riding over. And if there was any trouble along the way, something unexpected, he'd always hang fire for a second or two, getting his plan all thought out before he'd give an order. The air would be full of arrows and lead, but he'd just sit there on his damned mount, *thinking*. It was one of those times he got hit, on account of his hand was stuck up in the air

38

like a sign board while he figured out what to do with the men who was halted behind him. Maybe it wasn't the best way of doing things, but it was his.

After a while he said, "If they've been riding west for two days, it could be they've been working a placer claim up in the Black Hills. That's as likely a spot as any for them to have found their gold, but what're they doing heading out of there just now? They must have been holed up there all winter, and now when the streams will be fresheting, and the sand will have more gold in it than a Mexican's teeth, they head west."

"Maybe they need more supplies."

"Supplies, my grandmother. They didn't have to ride this far for supplies, or this way, either. With the trails opening up, there'll be plenty of wagons heading for the mines, or they could have gone down to Laramie."

"They just have two mules, too. No pack animals."

"How much gear?"

"Not much, Captain. Saddlebags and blanket rolls, that's all. They're traveling light."

"And hard."

"You're thinking they left some trouble wherever they got that gold?"

"Maybe they jumped somebody's claim late last year, got stuck in the mountains over the winter, and lit out early before the owners got back up there."

"But that kid don't look like no claim-jumper, Captain. Nor no thief. He looks more like a preacher, with that long hair of his. And he sure has the manners of one. Polite as pie."

"Some pies are polite until you cut into them," he said. "Besides, why is Jones breaking his back to be nice to him? That's not his style."

"You think they're in cahoots?" I said. "Jones and a *nigger?*"

"That's just my point. From what you say, Jones has already swallowed a number of what he would consider slights to his honor, and yet those two are still standing around alive."

39

"Maybe he's got one of his little jokes up his sleeve. That's what I thought, anyway, all the time he was smiling at the boy when he would of been letting light and air into another man saying those things to him."

"Could be," said the Captain, and knocked out his pipe.

"Maybe I should get on over there and see what's happening."

"Maybe you should," he said, which I took as an order.

But I hadn't no more than got up from my chair when he says, "How's the Judge this morning?"

"Well, to tell the truth, Captain, he's in one of his moods. Just stared at his food and then went back to his window."

"So it goes. Maybe you'd better get back over to the picket line."

"You don't reckon the Judge seen them coming into town?"

"If he noticed one of them was black, do you think he'd still be up there at the window?"

"No, sir, I guess not." I started out the door, but the Captain stopped me again, holding up his hand.

"Take a quarter out of the can and buy yourself a good breakfast."

"I already ate," I said. "I grub where I stay."

"I know that, Winky. But Bradley serves two things, and I'd rather you spend some of your time over there swallowing a little of the other."

Well, I took his quarter. Bradley's Injun made about the best bear sign in the Territory, gold-brown and spicy, so I figured I'd while away some time putting down a batch, a ground-layer as you might say for the kid's whiskey.

But she hadn't cooked up any, and Bradley said she wasn't going to. "Listen," he said, "if the smell of doughnuts goes out the galley pipe, we'll have the other half of town in here. I'm happy with my share, and I ain't about to advertise for more."

So I didn't get no bear sign, and had to settle for a can of sardines and some soda crackers, which I ate off the bar. Jones and the kid was still standing up there, talking, but everybody else was sitting around the stove, working hard at putting away the kid's whiskey, singing and laughing. It was noisy in there, but I didn't have no trouble hearing what they was saying. The kid was more or less hollering, having taken on a trifle too much whiskey, it looked like, and was shouting about their claim back in the hills, and what a lucky strike it had been, all on account of that lucky nigger, only it turns out he wasn't really a nigger, but an African.

You see, the kid's folks was Baptist missionaries, and they had found this little black baby over there in Africa, which had been left out in the jungle to die, on account of he was deaf and dumb. So Blondie's folks had taken him in to raise with their own child, and then when they left off missionarying on account of being killed by the Africans for doing it, Blondie and the little nigger, Ham, was sent by the other missionaries back to Ohio, where there was an uncle living on a farm there.

Well, the uncle raised them both up as if they was his own children, and sent little Ham to a school where he could learn the deaf and dumb signs, and the kid learnt it too, so they could talk together. They growed up on this farm, and had planned to be farmers theirselves, but then the news of the gold strikes come through, and the kid catched a sudden itch to travel. The nigger said it would mean good luck for them both, so they packed up and lit out for the Black Hills. The uncle didn't want them to go, but there wasn't no way of stopping them, short of tying them down. The nigger led them to this place where the sand was glittering with the stuff, way back up in a canyon that nobody had ever seen before, and they worked all last summer and all fall, and had kept on working that claim till the snow catched them and they had to stay up there all winter. But now they had all the gold they needed, and was heading west. The kid looked like Jones was supposed to ask what for, but what Jones asked was this:

"Ain't you worried traveling with all that gold?"

The kid just laughed. "As long as Ham is with me, I guess I don't have to worry," laughing some more, and then going on to tell a story about what old Ham done to some roughs which had tried to stop them back on the road a ways. And all they wanted was their mules, not knowing about the gold, of course. The kid said that Ham couldn't hear none or talk, but he had senses which took the place of ears, and was in some ways even better. The same powers which took them where the gold was could do lots of other things. If you tried to sneak up on Ham or bushwhack him, he knew about it almost the same time you did. Or if you lost something, you only had to ask old Ham where it was, and he'd find it for you. He could point to buried things, too, and witch for water. He could even tell fortunes, if he was of a mind to do it.

Well, Jones begun to get restless. I could see he thought the kid was pulling his leg, and a leg-puller like Fiddler Jones don't much cotton to that. He'd rather be out-and-out insulted than joshed. So he said, "I reckon I'd like to see that. Blondie, why don't you go out there and fetch that magic nigra of yours, and while you're at it, I'll give this silver dollar to one of the boys. Then we'll see if he can find it out."

Blondie laughed some more and went out, and Jones tossed the dollar to Willie Rogers, and Rogers dropped it into his boot with a wink, so as to show everybody how thick things was betwixt him and Fiddler Jones.

I looked over at Bradley to see if he would put up any fuss over the nigger coming into his saloon which he had already throwed out, but he was looking towards the door like everybody else.

Back come Blondie, Ham trailing right behind, and I seen his face for the first time. He was tired out, but a pleasant enough looking nigger, with a wide, open face, not all scowls and stubbornness like some you see. Especially since the War, you know, which give them a lot of fool notions about their worth. Used to be a nigger *knew* what he could bring, in dollars and cents, and that kept him satisfied and quiet, but all this freedom just brought on dissatisfaction and uneasiness, with a nigger thinking he was worth a whole lot but not able to find anybody who could give him an exact figure. This Ham was different. You could tell he was proud of hisself, walking high even though he was wore out, on account of being allowed into a white man's saloon, instead of being all upset because he was kept outside for so long. He'd been raised right, you could tell.

Then Blondie begun talking sign language to him, and Ham got very serious-looking, like a nigger will when you give him some little thing to do and he acts like he's hanging on every word you say, only he's likely to come back in about ten minutes and ask you to tell him all over again. It's their way, and you can't learn them any different.

While Blondie was waggling at him, old Ham kept his eyes moving around, first over at Jones and then all over the doggery. He give a nod every now and then, so as to show he understood, but I couldn't see how he could be looking around so and still keep an eye on Blondie's hands, which he would have to do if he wanted to know what was being said. When the kid had got done with semaphoring, Ham just give a last nod, and then started walking around the saloon, sort of winding his way amongst the fellers, who all set stock-still looking down into their glasses as if that was where the dollar was hid. He didn't go straight to Rogers, but he ended up there. He pointed to old Willie and smiled back at the kid.

Tolerable discussion followed, you might say, and it was a long while before you could hear Fiddler Jones, who was trying to holler something. Finally the noise died down enough so you could hear him. "Where has he got it hid?"

"He'll show you," said the kid. "But everybody has to keep quiet. He can't work where there's lots of noise."

"Hah!" said Jones. "You said he was deaf!"

The kid was very patient and calm, like Jones was some kind of ignoramus. "He *is* deaf, but something happens when everybody is talking at once. He gets very nervous."

That was true enough. The nigger was still standing next to

Willie Rogers, but his eyes kept dancing around and he kept rubbing his hands up and down the sides of his britches, like they was sweaty.

Well, everybody shushed up, and the kid signals to Ham some more, and the nigger he nods and looks down hard at Rogers and Rogers looked over at Jones like a dog taking a crap, and then Ham smiled and pointed down at the boot.

"It's in his boot, isn't it?" said the kid, with a little laugh.

A kind of grunt went around the room and Willie turned pale. He tried to reach down into his boot to get the dollar out, but he couldn't reach it with his fingers, so he had to take the boot off to get it, and was sweating considerable by then. He tossed the dollar to Jones with a sickly sort of smile, like it was *his* fault the nigger knew where the money was, and Jones caught it in the air without even looking at him, and then quick as a whip he snapped it back to the nigger. You couldn't see it, nor could you see the nigger's hand, neither, but out she went like a lizard's tongue, and that dollar landed in his palm with a smack you could hear all over the room.

"Give him a drink," Jones said to Bradley. "And no back-talk." You could see he was riled, but he was keeping it all behind his teeth, which was grinning. He looked somewhat like a constipated ape. You see, Jones had thought the kid was joking him, and he thought he was going to call Blondie's bluff, but when it turned out that it wasn't no joke, he got even madder than he would have got if it had been. Jones was that way. You couldn't ever tell what he was going to do next. The day before he might of laughed in the kid's face, and tomorrow he might shoot off the kid's kneecap.

Blondie come smiling up to him and said, Thanks all the same, that marvelous nigger never touched alcohol, but if Bradley had got any candy, why, he'd go for that. Sugar was his weakness.

"You got any candy, Bradley?"

"I dunno. I dunno," Bradley said. He was getting a trifle pale hisself. That African's little magic act had shook everybody up considerable, even the Injun, who was standing behind the bar, holding a plate of steak and eggs which the kid had ordered and chewing on her old gums as if there was something between them she wanted to put down quick. The eggs already had a little crust on them the way fried eggs will if they get to cooling, but the Injun just stood there, eyes shiny and black as drops of fresh tar.

Well, Bradley snatched the plate away and give her a boot in the ass to move her out of the way, and begun to scratch around here and there under the bar like a worried squirrel. Nobody said a word the whole time. The nigger stood right where he was, sort of blank-looking, and the kid was smiling, and Jones had on something that was supposed to be a smile but which was more like death, and everybody else in the room looked like it *was* death and they was the immediate family.

Finally Bradley come up with a tattery little sack of horehounds. "I got these," he said. "My wife . . ."

"Gimme," said Jones, and he took the sack and tossed it to the nigger. "Tell him Thanks."

"He knows."

"Then tell him he can vamoose."

But the nigger knew that, too, because he was already on his way, the kid having handed him the plate of steak and eggs to celebrate with. You could tell that was one happy nigger. All that gold they had between them wasn't nothing compared to a real silver dollar and them horehounds. He waved for the kid to come along with him to share the food and the rest, but all he got was a headshake No. Ham stopped dead in his tracks, then, and waggled a few signals with his free hand, and he wasn't smiling now. But the kid just shook that blond head again, and old Ham begun to scowl.

"Better run along, kid," said Jones. "Your nigger's calling."

Blondie didn't pay Jones no heed either, but told Bradley to order up another plate of steak and eggs. Ham give up waggling and come over to where the kid was standing. He put his big hand on his friend's arm and pulled at it, just a slight tug. Blondie turned around and give him a smile, but said No with another headshake, and pointed to the nigger's plate and to the door. Ham stood there looking down at the floor for a long minute, and then he turned and went out. But you could tell he wasn't happy about the arrangement.

Jones stood there taking it all in like a man looking at the sole of a new boot which just stepped into some cowshit, but he didn't open his mouth except to pour a glass of whiskey into it. Well, I was with the nigger. If that kid had any sense, Ham wouldn't of gone out the door alone. It was time to pick up winnings and haul freight, even if it meant sharing that meal on muleback. Jones was all hunched up like an outlaw mustang waiting for you to relax so he can uncoil and send you flying. But Blondie was either too tired to see how things were, or else too full of whiskey and a sense of blind luck to know better than to keep in the game now they was ahead, and just started in again, like before, telling all about how they most nearly starved up there in that canyon of theirs, the shanty being nothing more than a pile of logs and sods. The kid said the snow got so deep they had to dig a hole so the smoke could find a way out.

Jones had took up the kid's little shammy bag and while Blondie was talking and talking, he kept hefting it in his palm with a soft pat-a-pat sound, which got Bradley edgy. He come round and tried to take it away, slylike, as if it was a second or a third thought, but Jones looked up at him in such a way that he had a fourth thought and went on down the bar to where he come from, by the galley door where you could hear the kid's steak sizzling. After a while Jones undid the pucker strings and peered in with one eye, like a crow or magpie will do, and then he spit on a finger and poked it in and worked it around, like there was more deviled ham inside. Jones held that golden finger up to the light and admired it, his old yaller eyes fairly crossed, like a cat admiring a bird. Then he sort of swashed his finger clean in his whiskey and drunk it down, goldy glitter and all.

Blondie didn't say a word about Jones wasting the gold, didn't even seem to notice it, but went clattering on, as if Jones was powerful interested in hearing all about what happened up there in the mountains, and went right on, telling about the bones of the deer they had found, still standing up in the snow, where the wolves had got to them and eaten them down to the snowline, but the rest hadn't been touched, so when the spring come there they was—half bone and half rotted meat. The kid told how quiet it was deep down in their little hut under the snow, while the storm was howling way above them, how there would be a little moan come down the smoke hole, along with considerable smoke, but that was the only sound, and how it must be like that when you're dead and buried.

Blondie said they could talk in signs, but that wasn't the same as hearing another voice, and hearing only your own sounds about drove you loony. Besides, the nigger was as black as the rest of that place, and wasn't no more company than a shadow, so if it hadn't been for a book they had, the kid would of gone crazy. Blondie said that reading a book is like listening to a man talk, and this particular book, which they had found in a cabin along the way, all mouse-chawed and dirty, was a godsend in more ways than one, more of that nigger's good medicine.

Blondie pulled the book out of a jacket pocket, and a sorrier-looking godsend I never see. The kid begun to flip through the pages, admiring it and making noises over it, like a sharp drummer will do with something he wants you to get curious about, but Jones never paid no heed. He just kept jouncing the little bag in his hand, pat-a-pat-pat, and looking down at it with his head cocked back, like a man does that wears bifocals.

"How many more of these you got on you?" he asked.

"Just that one," said the kid.

"Where's the rest of it at? Cached up in the hills some-wheres?"

Blondie laughed. That kid was a great one for laughing.

"Why would I leave it up there, when I'm heading in the other direction?"

Jones didn't laugh, but he smiled a bit, rolling the bag around in his fingers. "Now, Blondie, don't you know it ain't polite to answer a question with another one?"

"It isn't?" asked the kid, like a schoolgirl who has just been told the same. I never see *such* blowed-in-the-glass innocence in all my born days. "Well, Ham has got the rest on him. He's stronger than me, you know."

Somehow the bag had broke open in Jones's hand, and a little runlet spurted out between his fingers and down onto the bar. "The nigger is carrying all your gold? *All* of it?"

"Well, it's *our* gold, and besides, he found it."

"You're mighty trusting of that nigger," Jones said. "Mighty fond of him, too, ain't you?"

"Like a brother," Blondie said, giving another of them laughs. "I already told you about that."

"So you did," said Jones. He dropped the busted sack, which was about empty anyways, into the pile of dust on the bar, and then brushed his fingers off onto the rest. It was a pretty sight, shiny yaller against the red-brown stain, and it was a shame that old Bradley come scuttling down and swept it up and put it into another bag so quick as he done.

"So you did," said Jones once more. "Mr. Bradley, when you're done tidying up, how about waltzing that bottle around once more? Unless maybe Blondie objects to wasting some more of his dust on us poor white folks. . . ."

"I don't object," said the kid. "Why . . . ?"

"You hear that, Mr. Bradley? Blondie don't mind. He loves white folks just as much as black. Start pouring."

So I got some whiskey at last, along with all the rest, but there wasn't any healths drunk on that round, nor on any of the others Blondie paid for. It was mighty stiff in there, like wet leather that's dried, and more than one man had drawed his seat closer to the door, even if it meant moving away from the stove. Bradley was always the peacemaker when it looked like his property was in danger, and he begun to hint that there might be an empty bed upstairs after all, and perhaps the kid could use a little nap before moving on to wherever it was they was going.

"Oregon," said Blondie, even though Bradley hadn't exactly asked. "We're heading for Oregon, but we'll be back."

Just then the Injun come out with Blondie's breakfast, which Bradley served up with the news that he just remembered there was some clean straw out back in his stall, and if the nigger didn't mind sharing it with his wife's mare, who was a gentle creature—the mare, he meant—why he didn't object to Ham taking a few winks hisself back there.

"That's why we're riding so hard," the kid said, digging into his steak. "The herders say if you don't get going early, you won't make it back in time."

"Herders?" said Bradley, and he looked as if he was a preacher and the kid had just swore.

Jones didn't even bat one of his yaller eyes. He just looked over at the kid very slow and then long and hard. "Back *where?*" he asked.

"Why, *here!*" Blondie said, after swallering a big mouthful of meat and eggs. "I mean, not here in town, but out there—on the range," waving towards the door with a fork and laughing some more. I did wish the kid would stop that. It wasn't the laugh so much, it was more the occasion.

"That's cow range," said Jones.

"Not any more, it isn't. The cows are all dead, on account of the winter."

"Thanks for the news," said Bradley, who was getting more and more nervous and edgy.

"We can get more," Jones said. "There's plenty dogies in Texas looking for a new home."

"There's plenty of room here, too," Blondie said, trying to eat and talk too. "Besides, this country was meant for sheep.

They've got heavy coats and can bunch together. You can build shelters for them and get them through winters worse than this one. There's no sense in bringing in more cows, don't you see? They'll just die off again, come the next bad winter."

"Tell us more," says Jones, and you felt he really wanted to hear. He had his yaller eyes fixed on the kid's face as if it was *his* plate of eggs and steak and he was waiting for somebody to hand him a knife and fork. I wasn't even sure he would wait for the fork.

III

Funny thing, but when that blond kid first begun to talk, people was sitting around the saloon every which way, but it wasn't long before you noticed they was shifting around in their seats, or hitching up a bench, or changing their place on the wall, and pretty soon they was a regular audience. The kid seen it, too, and begun to throw a few words in their direction, and then left off with Jones and just talked to the others, maybe giving Jones a quick look every now and then to let him know he wasn't entirely forgot. Now I maybe was wrong about that kid being deaf and dumb, but I sure was right about the preacher part. Blondie was bred pure, and that dead missionary would of been right proud to own up to his child.

Not that the kid was talking about God and the Bible and all that righteous crap, because those boys wouldn't of stood for it. No, it was money-talk they was getting, and there wasn't a better congregation for that kind of gospel anywheres. They was cowboys to a man, and the kid was talking sheep, but you got to remember that this was way back before the troubles in

'92, and most folks around Wyoming hadn't formed any opinions one way or other. And even if they had, the kid was mighty convincing. I was into my second can of sardines when Blondie begun, and next thing I knew I was scratching Bradley's old cat behind the ears while she licked up the oil she had saved for dessert. Now that was the first time I ever left off eating a can of sardines before I was finished, and it wasn't only that the kid was a spellbinder, but I couldn't shake the notion I had heard it all somewheres before.

Blondie was waving that godsend book around, for all the world like one of them pocket testaments which Frisco street preachers carry, and was quoting chapter and verse to us without checking the text, only flipping pages back and forth, because it was all got to heart, you see, and those bright blue eyes never left the crowd. They was all attention, every man-Jack of them, slurping up the talk about quick profits and the wool bonanza. Those was the kid's very words, the "wool bonanza," and they had come out of the little book, along with the rest, and stuck in my mind like a bit of thorn can catch in your sock, scratching your foot but you can't seem to find it no matter how hard you look. While everybody else was hanging on Blondie's words, and could see them bales and bales of golden wool moving out of town on freight cars, I kept fussing like a dog with a flea, trying to remember where I had heard them exact words before.

Well, that Blondie was a holy wonder, and had the Midas touch for sure, changing the whole damn territory into gold right before their eyes. The grass in Wyoming was gold, the harvests was gold, and even the goddam *sheep* had gold hooves, according to that marvelous book before us. Blondie was particular fond of a proverb which was in the book, a Spanish saying, "Wherever the foot of the sheep touches, the land turns to gold."

"Shit!" said Jones, after the kid had rolled out that proverb for the fifth or sixth time.

Well, it broke like a fart at a prayer meeting. Everybody had more or less forgot old Fiddler was standing back there at the bar, and even Blondie was shook up some, and broke off in the middle of the next sentence to look back at him.

"Shit, not gold," Jones said, as soon as they was all looking at him. "That's how it ought to read, kid: Wherever the foot of the sheep touches, the land turns to *shit*."

The kid just stood there and stared at him. It was like Jones had displayed his pecker to the congregation, which he wasn't above doing, but that's another story.

"And that ain't out of no book. You ask anybody from Texas what sheep does to the range, and he'll tell you the same. You claim a sheep is all meat and wool, but I'll tell you what your goddam sheep is—all eating and shitting, that's what. He'll chew your forage right down to the roots, and then he'll shit on what's left and stomp it down so hard you'll break a damn plowshare on it. A sheep's worse than a fucking locust, which will at least leave something to grow, but a lousy sheep! They act like they ain't never coming back, and where they've been only sagebrush and cactus will ever grow again."

Well, none of us had ever seen old Jones carry on so. It wasn't like him to get all hot under the collar like that. It wasn't his style. We was flabbergasted, everyone in that saloon, and just held our breath, wondering if we was in for a earthquake or would get off easy with a tornado.

Not Blondie, who had already begun to fidget, and when Fiddler stopped to take on some whiskey, that book begun to flutter around like a bird that's flew in the window and wonders what ever happened to the sky.

"But Texas is *flat*, and Wyoming is *hills*. Right in the book it tells how Wyoming is ideal for sheep grazing, with its hard, porous, gravelly soil, and the bright equable climate and the dry, bracing atmosphere. Right here it says how sheep and cattle can share the same range, with the cattle in the lowlands and the sheep up on the hills. Why, it says that the time will come when we will have both shepherds and shepherdesses, man and wife, and that the patriarch, as of old, with his sons, daughters, and his sons' wives and daughters will follow the herds, crook in hand. It's all there in the book, about how healthy the climate is, for man and beast alike."

Jones was so mad he couldn't keep his eyes steady, but kept them moving around the room, looking at nobody or nothing. "Healthy!" he said. "Healthy!" He pointed out the window. "Ask them cows how healthy it is!"

"But I already told you," said the kid, very calm and patient, "sheep are different. . . ."

"Oh, yes," said Jones, laughing out loud. "Yes, I reckon sheep *are* different, and so are sheepherders." He laughed some more, only it was more like a bark, and pushed himself off from the bar. "I had you classed all wrong, Blondie. I thought you was a nigger-lover, but you're something worse. You're a goddam *sheep*lover, which is only a notch above a *pig*-lover!" He was talking to the kid, but he stepped up and leaned forward at the cowboys, like an actor will, you know, and when he was done speaking he laughed again, as if it was a joke, and a couple others in the saloon joined in, mostly out of habit.

Those few laughs done Jones a heap of good. You could see it was like Doc Kingsbury's tonic, which the Captain says is half alcohol, half laudanum. He seemed to calm right down, and got a dreamy look and begun to smile a little. Some of the cowboys took this to be a good sign, and sighed and shifted around in their chairs, but not me.

"Our Savior was a shepherd," said Blondie, in a quiet voice.

"That's right, He was," said Jones. "And if He had stuck to carpentering, He might of lived considerable longer, wouldn't He?" Jones laughed some more, and this time half the saloon joined in. "But jest like Old Abe, He had to go mess around with something that wasn't none of His concern. Jesus should of stuck to carpentering, and Abe should of stuck to telling dirty jokes."

Well, Blondie had done a lot of laughing before, but not any longer. Everybody in the doggery was guffawing and whooping, but the kid didn't seem in the mood any more.

"That's all right, kid," Jones said. "You read us some more from that book. Maybe you'll convince me yet."

Blondie was looking sober as an undertaker with a bad case of piles. "Doubting Thomas laughed, too, but he ended up a martyr."

"Oh, no," Jones said. "I ain't *ending up* for no sheep, not me. That Thomas feller must of been a shepherd, dropping his pants for some old black ram!" Fiddler stuck his ass-end around and shook it just in case you didn't get what he was driving at, which everybody had, except maybe the kid.

"I meant he came to doubt and stayed to believe."

"What's that?" Jones said, cupping his ear like a deaf man. "Came in doubt and paid to relieve?"

"*B*elieve."

"Oh, I be*lieve*," Jones said. "I *believe*, all right. If that book of yours says a herder will die a rich man, I *believe* it." He looked round the room and give a general wink to all. "Half of it, anyways." Jones pointed up to the medals around his sombrero. "There's the proof."

Well, everybody was having a good time by now except Blondie, who had lost the congregation to the devil hisself. For a while there it looked like there was going to be some converts to the sheep religion, but Fiddler Jones had broke the spell. Not that them cowboys necessarily believed what Jones had to say, just that they was following him out of old habits. You can bet that some of them was doing some thinking in the backs of their heads about what the kid had said, even while they was laughing along with Jones.

Maybe Blondie sensed that, or just seen that Jones had the advantage now, and there wasn't no profit in staying in the game. However it was, the kid done the best possible with a bad thing, setting down the book and picking up the whiskey glass, putting on a smile so as to be a good sport about it. Jones had the floor and was going to keep it, maybe even take it home with him. He was getting off a general speech about sheep and their ways and herders and *their* ways, which was all tied up together with the differences between white sheep and black. I don't know where Jones got his information, but it sure as hell wasn't ever printed in no book.

We was all laughing, of course, and pretty soon even Blondie joined in, because old Fiddler *was* damned funny, you know, not just with words but with hisself as a whole, you might say. Sometimes a look or a twist of his face would set you laughing. I wasn't sure the kid understood all the jokes, because most people in the same spot would of had to take Jones up on one or two of them, but Blondie just stood right there at the bar smiling and laughing now and then while Fiddler got more and more outrageous. Jones seen it, and worked his way over so he could once in a while reach out and muss the kid's hair, or give a little poke in the shortribs, all in fun you see, like Blondie was his best friend and would understand how all the joshing wasn't meant for meanness but just for fun. Jones was that way, like I've said. He could get you laughing at your mother's funeral, telling jokes about her bad performance in bed.

Well, I was laughing along with the rest, from time to time sucking what oil the cat had left in the sardine can off my finger, but there was something about Jones's handling and jostling that kid made me uneasy. It was for all the world like a cannibal and a missionary, who was putting up with all that skylarking and poking until a good time come to pick up the Bible again, having no idea that the cannibal had other plans, and that all his touchings was only to get a feel and judge how big a pot he was going to need, and how long the water was going to have to boil. Because Jones was working up to some kind of outrage, I was sure of it. All that talk about sheep, and the nigger waiting by the door, had gone to work on him, and mischief was working up inside, like hot water in one of them

56

geysers. I hadn't ever seen him go about things in such a fashion before, but there wasn't no telling about Fiddler Jones. He had more styles of troublemaking than a mule.

Right in the middle of it all, that big nigger come strolling in, bold as brass and twice as shiny, and lays a hand on Blondie's arm, like before, only his scowl was heavier than ever, a regular thundercloud. It wasn't one of those useless darky's frowns, sulky and stubborn, but what you might call an *African* look, with a ring through its nose, or a bone. The cannibal in the Mexican hat seemed to have met his match for once, because the nigger didn't waste no time wiggle-waggling, but just turned and walked back out of there, carrying the kid with him under one arm.

Well, wasn't old Jones a study! He broke off halfway through a joke, and just stood there like a man who has had a express train take a short cut through his dining room in the middle of a fifteen-minute blessing, and him just beginning to warm up while his dinner was getting cold. You never see the like. It most made you feel sorry for him, being cut off in the glory of his fun like that, left with nothing to hang the rest of it on but empty air, and what come to mind was a man I once knew who had an old whore die under him and he had already paid for the full night.

When Jones finally got his wind back he used it to whistle with—a long, dying sound it was, like a steamboat way down the next bend. Then he hoisted off his sombrero and hoed about in that amazing briar patch of his, keeping both eyes on a crack in the boards about two feet from his boots. While all this was going on, nobody said a word and hardly nobody moved. You could hear Bradley's Injun snoring in the kitchen as clear as if she was right here in the room.

"Well," said Jones, in a long drawl. "Well, I'll–be–dipped–in–shit!"

They all laughed then, like it was the funniest thing they'd heard in years, holding on to one another and roaring till tears come running down their cheeks. They laughed so hard and so long the Injun woke up and come shuffling out to see what it was all about, standing there in the doorway to the kitchen with her old wrinkled prune of a face peering at us, and with no more chance of figuring it out than a desert turtle understands the stage that just knocked him ass-over-teakettle.

All the time they was laughing, Jones just stood there, scratching and scratching his head, until a little snow of dandruff come falling down on his shoulder, his face all screwed up in the damnedest look ever, like he had just seen a cow walk downstairs. Finally, when all the ruckus died, he jammed his hat back on and give a sniff or two, wiping under his nose with a finger, and still looking at nobody or nothing, hitched up his britches and said to Bradley, "Before Blondie left us, didn't he call for drinks all round?"

There was a general cheer went up, and old Bradley got busy again with his bottle, happy to get a little more of the kid's custom while their gold was still there. Because anybody could plainly see that Blondie's lucky nigger had got second thoughts.

Their precious book was still laying on the bar too, and I said to nobody in particular, "I guess he'll be wanting this," and since nobody in particular said anything to me, I just picked it up and walked out with it.

Right outside the door they was, waggling at each other like a piece of tangled string was in between and there was a contest to see who could get it untangled first. Ham would just get started, and the kid would brush his hands away, and start in, only to get knocked out of the game by the nigger, who would try to finish what *he* had begun, the both of them shaking their heads at each other and scowling.

There didn't seem to be any sense in butting in just then, so I took a peek into that marvelous book to pass the time, but hadn't no more than seen who wrote it before I lit out across the planks to the jailhouse, quick-march-double-time.

"Look here!" I said. "Look at *this*, will you!"

I held the book under the Captain's nose and shook it at him, but he didn't even look at it.

"I thought you were supposed to be over at Bradley's place, watching the goings-on. . . ."

"Damn it all, Captain, sir, this *is* the goings-on," I said. "This is where the kid got all his damn-fool notions about sheep and gold and all the rest of that truck he's been peddling."

"What in hell are you talking about?" he said. "I told you to take it easy on the whiskey."

"I ain't had but one glass of whiskey since I left here," I said. "I been mostly sharing sardines with Bradley's goddam cat and listening to a lot of damn-fool nonsense and wondering where I heard it all before, and *this* is where!" I give the book a shake or two more, and the Captain took it, and read what I had read.

"Brisbin!" he said. "For sweet Jesus' sake."

"He's gone and wrote a damn *book*, Captain, and put in all them crazy notions of his, and that kid has been reading it, and what's worse, he believes it!"

"Slow down, Winky," the Captain said, holding up his hand. "You got to remember, now, I don't know anything more than you knew an hour ago."

"Yes, sir," I said. "And I'm trying to tell you, only . . ."

Up went his hand again. "Now, first off, where did you get this book?"

"Why," I said, "over at Bradley's. Off the bar, where the kid left it."

"Then he's gone? The both of them?"

"No, sir, they ain't gone, but if the nigger had had *his* way, they would of been, a half-hour since. They're outside Bradley's right now, arguing. The kid wants to stay."

"Fiddler Jones have anything to do with it?"

Well, there wasn't nothing for me to do except start in from the beginning, pretty much like it happened, only quicker, but

I hadn't only just got to the part about the sheep and all, when in walks Blondie, stiff as starch.

"That is my book, I believe," the kid says, staring down where the Captain is still holding it open with his thumb.

The Captain was very cool and proper. He got up slow and handed the book to the kid with a nice smile, like it was a Sunday-school prize. "Yes," he said, "my deputy here borrowed it to show me. Your book seems to have been written by a former associate of ours, and my deputy appears to have overlooked the formal rules of etiquette in his desire to bring me the news."

Well, you should of seen that kid melt, like butter on hot griddle cakes, all sweetened by the Captain's syrup. "You're a friend of General Brisbin?"—as if Brisbin was a Territorial governor, or somebody important.

"We have followed the guidon together," said the Captain, and nothing but the kid has got to shake his hand, which was the one which the General must of shook, which it wasn't, but the other one, which the Captain had lost, all so excited and pleased you would of thought the Captain might be ashamed, knowing what he really thought of old Brisbin. But no, the Captain kept right on.

"I knew him," he says, "before he was a famous author."

That was back in the winter of '71, more than fifteen years before, when the Captain was just a second lieutenant, in charge of a troop of horse which was to escort a bunch of miners on their way up to Atlantic City, near the South Pass region. Lo was acting up back then, still, on account of the mines was too close to the Shoshone reservation. The Government had built a fort in Smith's Gulch, just outside Atlantic City, and stuck a couple infantry companies there to keep the Injuns happy, but they wasn't content even then. They left the town alone, but kept pestering the trails so bad the miners kicked up a row and the Government give in and let them have mounted protection every now and then, especially after some unimportant little massacre that wasn't nothing more than a few young bucks out to earn their eagle feathers.

That's how the troubles always started on the Border—with miners. Back right after the War, when General Sherman took command, the problem was the miners taking short cuts through Powder River country, which Lo had been told was his for keeps, and fought like the very devils of Hell to keep it, knowing most likely it was his last stand, and the only good land left him and a place of powerful medicine, too. Lo maybe had a doom on him, but he didn't act like he knew it, you had to say that for him. There was a lot of people said it was Providence, that the Injun had to go to make way for civilization, and there was considerable soldier-boys anxious to help Providence along, having seen their friends laying about without no hair and sometimes with no head and other parts too. You see, Lo believed that if you was all in pieces when you died you would have a awkward time of it later on. They could do some mighty ugly things to a dead man, and to a man before he died, too. If it was your friend they done it to, why, it was only natural to want to do it right back to them, only in spades.

Take it all around, Lo was a filthy savage, with the brain of a coyote and the virtues to match. But it did seem to me Lo had got some rights, dirty and ornery and ugly as he was, and that there was a line to be drawed somewheres. A deal is a deal, even with an Injun. That damned Powder River country which Red Cloud was so hot under his buckskins about wasn't particular choice land, not back then it wasn't. It was just a place between a bunch of miners and what they hoped was their gold. And of course "ye editor" in Cheyenne and Laramie was screaming bloody murder for the Army to move in troops to protect those miserable sons-a-bitches, on account of more soldiers meant more business for Wyoming.

A lot of fortunes was made back then, but not many by the miners. The ones who got rich was those with ox teams and wagons who trucked supplies north to the forts. And the men who got killed trying to hold them forts which was eventually give back to Red Cloud, why, they was part of the cost, only they ain't on nobody's ledgers. The funny thing was, the soldiers who didn't get killed mostly blamed the Injuns, when all Lo was trying to do was keep what had been told him was his. So the soldiers done what they could to wipe Lo off the map and Lo done the same, while the freighters and merchants was getting richer and richer and the miners kept hurrying through like hogs on the way to their swill. The soldiers finally won and the Injuns lost, but they was both losers if you ask me.

If it had been up to me and the Captain, we would of just let the Injuns and the miners fight it out betwixt theirselves, and I don't think the miners would of lasted much past the second week. Nor would the freighters have made much profits hauling them supplies. If those editors wanted to run up north and give their beloved miners a helping hand, well, that would of been all right, too. It's a free country, like the editors are fond of saying. But the Captain and me, we didn't cotton much to the idea of riding herd on them miners. Your regular settler is one thing, whether he's a rancher or a herder or even a nester, but miners ain't planning on staying, on helping the country along. All they want is to take something out of the land without putting anything back. You couldn't help feeling the Injuns had the right on their side for once.

Because when it comes to being a greedy, ignorant savage, an Injun ain't got a patch on your miner, which is a dirty, foul-mouth, ornery bastard, always quarreling over a worthless patch of ground or drawing his gun over a bunch of iron pyrites. The Captain claimed that a miner is a human being with the outer wrapper tore away, leaving nothing but the nasty insides, like a rotten potato you have peeled by mistake. We all got some greed in us, but a miner is all greed, and everything he does can be explained by it. He don't wash because he's too busy digging in the dirt, and when he ain't digging he's swilling down food, cooked, raw, or still kicking, and when he ain't swilling, why, he's sliding around hoping to steal somebody's gold, food, or dry goods.

There's people who'll say that some miners have been caught in a brave act, but if you'll look closely at the thing, you'll always find greed somewheres. A miner will fight like a bearcat if you try to take away his gold or stick your spoon into his stew, and if he is on the way to a new strike, he'll chew his way through barb wire to get there. And once he has staked his claim, he'll fight tooth and nail to defend it. But hell, so will the weasel and the wolverine, two of the greatest goddam cowards, bullies, and low-down miserable sneaks there is in nature.

Like I said, the second most thing a miner prizes is his food, and when he's real hungry, he sometimes will put food first. Take away his grub for a day and he's mean as a badger. By the second day he'll eat bark and grass, and by the end of a week nothing soft is safe, and that includes his immediate family. He'll even give up working his claim long enough to bolt down his partner; if one'll turn his head long enough for the other to get the jump on him, which ain't very likely. But a hungry miner's favorite dish of humanity is an Injun, so you see the Shoshone wasn't so misplaced in their instincts.

I only say all this so you will understand what we was up against back there in the winter of '71–'72. You see, we had run smack into a blizzard on our way into South Pass, and once we got in there, we couldn't get back out. The snow kept coming and coming, and piled so high the Union Pacific couldn't get through, to say nothing of the stage or ox-teams. That blizzard would of ate a team whole. The miners got pretty hungry theirselves by the end of the week, and if Brisbin, who was commanding officer at the fort, hadn't broke out his own stores, the population would of become considerable more compact. Take what Alfred Packer done, all by hisself.

Packer was prospecting in the Colorado Rockies with some

other fellers, and they got snowed in. By the time a rescue party got in there, Packer had put away *five* other miners, and even a skinny miner has got as much meat on him as an antelope. The Captain figured that at the Packer rate of consumption, the six thousand folks in Atlantic City and South Pass City would of supplied only about one thousand of their fellow citizens, and the one thousand bereaved would of kept only two hundred mourners alive, and the two hundred dear departed would of taken care of only forty dearly beloveds, which would of been food for a scantling eight survivors. It was likely, when you consider the appetite of your average miner, that only one man would of been left by the end of the winter if Major Brisbin hadn't of interfered.

It ain't up to me to say he was wrong, but I wouldn't of done the same. It may be bad for one human being to eat another, but a miner is different, and somehow it seems all right to make a exception in their case. They sent Alfred Packer to prison for eating his ration of five, and to my way of thinking it wasn't justice. If I had been the judge, I'd of given Packer a gun and a skillet and sent him out to better hisself, and I'd of encouraged others to follow his example.

But the Major insisted on handing out his stores to the miners, and no one ate anybody that I knowed of. That's the kind of man he was, anyway, always thinking the best of everybody, no matter what kind of human skunk they was. Before the War he had been an Abolitionist and run a little antislave newspaper back in Pennsylvania. You couldn't really hold it against him, though. First of all, it was part of that goodness and generosity of his, and second, he joined up a private when the War broke out. Like the Captain said, a man who backs up what he says with his life can't be all that bad.

Somewhere along the way Brisbin picked up an officers' commission and three Confederate rifle balls. He got his first souvenir at the battle of Bull Run, another at Beverly's Ford, and the last at the Sabine Crossroads. There wasn't no doubt that he was a brave man, and a sincere man. I guess the final proof was in 1864, when they made him colonel of the Fifth Cavalry, which was niggers. The Government honored his bravery in other ways, too, and by the end of the War he was a brigadier general in the volunteers, which, when the War was over, boiled down to the rank of captain.

Well, by that time the Abolitionist cause had dried up and become the Republican Party, but Captain Brisbin kept right on writing. He done a campaign biography for General Grant and Mr. Colfax, while he was out on the Western frontier, in 1868, no more being able to stop writing than a miner can stop digging. He wasn't an Abolitionist any more, but that didn't hold him back none. You dam up a river and it'll pour over somewheres else. It *has* to. Some of the Abolitionists turned to Female Rights, but after Brisbin got done electing General Grant, he turned to cattle, sheep, and horses.

And he wasn't trying to *abolish* no more, he was trying to do just the opposite, but you could see the same old spirit at work, because how else can you explain a man who can give a bunch of snowbound soldiers a talk on the beautiful climate of Wyoming? A man who has just stomped ten foot of snow off his boots, and is standing in front of a fireplace with his backside smoking and his frontside still froze, and tells you that there ain't a better climate in the world for cattle, sheep, and horses. Sometimes the wind would be howling so down the chimney that he would have to shout.

Well, I don't mean to make fun of old Brisbin. He might of been a trifle loco, but he wasn't all the way there. Like the Captain said, he could see past all the fussy details that keep most men living ordinary lives. Maybe he stretched things a bit, but what difference did that make? Maybe he seen just what he wanted to see and looked right past what he didn't want to see, but so what? Maybe the Territories wasn't the best grazing ground in the world, but they *was* good pasture, and many a man has made a fortune there since, doing just what the Major said he should. The Captain said that Brisbin was a prophet. He said that not many prophets hit it right on the head, but what they don't have in aim, they make up with enthusiasm, and the nail does get drove home anyway. He said the art of prophecy ain't nothing more than plain old exaggeration.

Take the blizzard. For the most of us ordinary johnnies that blizzard was an important fact. We cussed that blizzard and cussed the fates that had took us into South Pass and cussed the politicians in Washington that had ordered us there. That blizzard seemed a sign that mankind wasn't never intended to inhabit the South Pass region, that it was meant for Injuns only, and they was welcome to it. We all prayed, to ourselves and out loud, that if the Almighty would only let us out of there, we wouldn't never come back. Except the Major.

Now the bare, cold fact of that blizzard never meant nothing to Brisbin. It wasn't part of his idea of the West, so he just ignored it, like a polite lady won't pay attention to a belch. He could look out over that great whiteness and see cows grazing off it. He looked at the snow like he once must of looked at the notion niggers wasn't fit to earn their own way in the world. It was a *fact* to us, but opinion to him. After all, he had his facts, whole notebooks full of them. It might of been twenty below that winter, but his facts told him that the mean average temperature for that season in Wyoming was between thirty and thirty-two above. Now what's a few weeks of twenty-below *opinion* to a *fact* like that?

The Major had it all figured out that there wasn't no difference worth mentioning betwixt the weather on the plains and what they had back East. If anything the Western weather was better. He said that the Great American Desert wasn't nothing but a lie—"myth" he called it—and that the soil was richer and the water sweeter than any place this side of Eden. He had seen or heard of fifty-pound cabbages, twelve-pound turnips, and three-pound potatoes growed right there on the fertile banks of the Cache-la-Poudre. The Captain said it was to his credit he didn't claim they grew on trees, but then he wasn't really creative except on the matter of cows.

Take the feed problem, which according to the Major wasn't. He said there wasn't no need to cut hay for winter feed on account of the grass cured right on the ground, and the grazing season went on through the winter. Not that he didn't take the snow into his calculations, but according to him it never amounted to more than three inches of light, powdery stuff, and it didn't lay on the ground for long, either, he said. Maybe he meant that it didn't snow more than three inches an *hour*, and that the reason it didn't lay on the ground for long was that it was usually busy piling itself into ten-foot drifts.

But feed didn't inspire him half so much as profits. My, how the idea of profits got him going, rolling out round figures like shiny new cartwheels. Herds, now, he generally give in even numbers—twenty thousand, fifteen thousand, ten thousand, five thousand. His mother must of been scared by an auctioneer, because he sure hated to split an even thousand. He was the same way with per cents. Profits from cows he reckoned at about twenty-five per cent, and he calculated sheep even higher, starting down around a starving rate of thirty-five per cent the first year, and then moving on up to forty-five per cent the second year, and sixty per cent the third year, nice even figures and percentages rattled off like a ticker-tape machine, and he could make your fortune in less than five minutes on nothing more than a scrap of paper.

"Take a herd of four hundred Texas cows," he would say, "worth five thousand dollars to begin with. At the end of one year the cows would have at least four hundred calves, each worth seven dollars. I count full yield"—that was always his way—"for in cross-breeding there is not one cow in a hundred that is barren; and if you provide hay and shelter, there isn't a loss of over one per cent of the calves dropped. Therefore your first year's profit will be four hundred calves, at seven dollars each, which amounts to a total of twenty-eight hundred dollars. And you've just begun. Because each year the old cows will go on breeding new calves at a value of seven dollars each. And by the fourth year, half of your original calves will be heifers, bearing calves of their own. When your fifth year comes around you will have two hundred steers to sell, each worth thirty dollars, giving you a *cash* profit of twenty-one thousand. And after the fifth year, your profits will be enormous. In eleven years you could, with care, be at the head of a blooded stock farm worth a hundred thousand, and very soon afterward be its sole owner."

Well, it was all there in that raggedy book, and it had all got inside Blondie's crazy head, and there wasn't nothing to do but sit there and hear it all over again, all about the glorious opportunities of the West. While Blondie was talking in that quiet little voice, I kept hearing the Major, too, bringing back memories of him lecturing to us soldiers while we was standing up to our asses in the snow. The Major worked on us for weeks but never won a single man over, but it did look like he had got hisself a disciple at last. Because this kid was just filled to the eyes with Brisbin's ideas, and they leaked out everywheres at once, like shot from a split cartridge.

The Captain listened for a while, maybe every now and then glancing through the book, and then he got up and put it into Blondie's hand, which happened to be stuck out to make some point or other, and taking holt of the scruff of the kid's sheepskin, he lifted the whole business, book and all, and set it outside the door on the boardwalk, which he then shut and threw the bolt on. Never once did the kid stop talking.

"My goodness," said the Captain. "Has he been carrying on like that all morning?"

"Yes, sir," I said. "Mostly, he has."

"Well," said he, touching his head a couple times, "that explains why Jones hasn't broken him over his knee for kindling. The boy is mad as a hatter."

"I figured as much," I said, and then went on to finish the story, about how Blondie started to read the book just to keep from going bughouse, but after a while it got to the kid, and then begun to work like cider, along with the loneliness and the darkness and the gold fever. "Pretty soon he got it all mixed up," I said. "The real gold he'd got under him there and that beef bonanza old Brisbin was always jingling and jangling like a sack of coins. And then the sheep and all and maybe what he'd remembered from the Bible, because he's a real Christer all right. . . ."

"So when spring came, he and that black man left a sure fortune behind them and headed for here."

"No sir, to Oregon, to buy sheep. Then they're coming back."

The Captain groaned a little. "And the boy of course confided all this to that Texan?"

"Yes, sir, and to anybody else who would listen."

"But the black wants to leave?"

"It appears so, yes."

"Then it looks like one of them has got some sense left."

"Yes, indeed he has, Captain," I said. "That nigger's got sense left to spare, and some that most of us don't have besides." Then I told him about the coin trick, and next about how he wasn't really a nigger but a African, which I hadn't done before, and how Blondie said he was good medicine and all.

"Yes," said the Captain, "I've heard about such things. Cheap magic-show clairvoyance tricks. They can be very convincing."

"That might be," I said. "But *who* are they trying to convince, Captain. And *why?* How come that medicinal African led them into Bradley's in the first place? What're they looking for?"

"Well, what they found was Fiddler Jones, and now the black man wants to lead them out again, and I believe he's on the right track."

"Yes, and how come that Blondie don't take his lucky nigger's advice, like he always done before, and haul his ass out of here?"

"That boy's crazy as a loon," said the Captain. "There's just no accounting for him."

"He don't have no patent on it," I said. "This town's a regular bughouse, it seems like. Maybe that's why the nigger brung him here in the first place, hoping like would love like. There's the Judge, to begin with, up there waiting for *his* nigger to show up, which most likely is dead long since, and then there's Bradley, over there giving out credit to deadbeats, hoping to get rich quick by going into debt, to say nothing of this whole damn town, sitting here waiting for a railway to run through it which will probably go five miles south. And what about Brisbin, an educated man, too! What about him?"

"I have a theory," said the Captain, who most usually did. "It's the space that gets to people out here. There's just too much *sky*, and people swell up like frogs in a vacuum jar. There's no holding them down."

"Yes," I said, "like that crazy gambler Sturgis, with all his wild talk about opportunities."

"A man like that back East might just have a little germ of madness somewhere in him that wouldn't ever really amount to anything, like most of us have deep down inside, like a shoot on a potato that's kept in a bag. But out here, things grow."

"Like Brisbin's fifty-pound cabbages," I said. "They're cabbage-heads, every damned one of 'em, from Brisbin to the boy."

"No," the Captain said, "the boy's different. It wasn't open space that drove *him* mad, it was a closed-in space, a nailed-in space, and it pressed him down, like solitary confinement or a premature burial. He's not like Brisbin, full of hope for the country. All he has is a small piece of that optimism, like most converts, and it has grown into a small, mean craziness. Sheep, just sheep."

"Like a miner," I said. "Only it's wool, not gold."

"It's all the same," the Captain said. "That boy's a miner at heart. He started out a miner and is a miner still, for all his talk about shepherds and sheep. He's a miner at heart, and a cannibal, like that black man with him. I thought it was Jones who would start trouble here, but I was wrong. Jones is an innocent

70

next to that pair. It's the boy and his electromagnetic African we've got to watch."

"That might be," I said, "but old Fiddler looks very hungry at that kid from time to time."

"What Jones doesn't realize is he can't count on dealing with the boy alone. He's like the tenderfoot who finds a bear cub and starts to tease and play with it, laughing at all the squealing and the grunting, and gets to laughing so hard he doesn't hear the mother bear coming until it's too late."

"You want we should lock 'em up, or run 'em out of town, or what?"

"Both, and even more. But we can't do anything except wait."

"It's for their own good, Captain," I said. "For everybody's good."

The Captain looked at me in such a way that I knew a quote was coming, and it come: " 'The General Good,' " he said, " 'is the plea of the scoundrel, hypocrite, and flatterer.' "

"That might be," I said, "but so long as those crazies is loose around here, we're in for trouble, and you know it and I know it."

" 'The noblest motive is the public good,' " he said.

"Yes, sir, Captain. I'll stand by that. I say run 'em out or lock 'em up, and I'll bet there's a poet around somewheres that said the same thing."

"Winky," he said, "there's only one poet that counts here, and he's the one who wrote: 'It is better that ten guilty persons escape than one innocent suffer.' "

"Who's that?" I said. "Shakespeare, or the Bible?"

"Blackstone."

"So we let them be."

"Until something happens, yes," he said. "There's no other way."

IV

When I got back over to Bradley's, things seemed to have simmered down. Outside, the nigger was where he had been left before, all folded up against the wall and asleep, it looked like, and the kid was back inside, only sitting down now and alone, quiet as could be. Fiddler Jones wasn't joking around now, but was just leaning against the bar watching the little gambler which we called Leland Stanford, who had took in his share of the kid's whiskey and was getting mighty confidential.

He had out his deck, as usual, and was tossing three-card monte, clattering away while he done it about how it was a fool's game every time, which most of us knowed anyways. He said there wasn't no money in the house except what the boy was spending, so it wouldn't do no harm to explain how the game was rigged. He said we shouldn't ever tell anybody who told us, though, because there was a league of gamblers which would track him down and kill him if they found out he spilled the beans. It was just like the Masons, he said. They had all took a oath, and what happened to Morgan wasn't a patch on what they would do to *him*.

"With three cards and one guess," he said, "it's two to one against you at the start, and when things get warm, why, we make a little adjustment to increase the odds." Then he held up three cards. "Here, gentlemen," he said, "you see the eight of clubs, the eight of spades, and the queen of hearts. The lady, gentlemen, is the winning card." He showed the cards to everybody and then shuffled them around, face down on the table, like it's always done, only maybe a little slower so you could keep track of the queen. Then he spread them wide, and asked Compson Price to point her out. Old Comp grinned like a ape and done so and he was right, but so would a child of been.

"Shit," he said. "That was easy. But if'n there had been money on the table, I reckon you'd of moved them cyards a little faster."

"Sure," said the little gambler. "But we always give away a few tricks at first to get you interested. *Now* watch." He picked up the three cards and away he went, only there wasn't a man in that room could tell where the queen was when he spread them out the second time. They moved so fast it was like a hummingbird's wings—a sort of blurry whip. "Okay," he says to Price. "Pick the lady out."

Price shook his head and grinned some more, only the ape wasn't feeling so spruce as before. "Shit," he said, and that was all.

"Don't know?" asked Leland Stanford. "Anybody know?" He looked around the room. "Nobody?"

"*I* know," said Fiddler Jones, and there was a little shuffling sound as people cleared a space betwixt him and the gambler, just in case. It was habit.

"Come on over and pick it up," said the gambler.

"I don't need to," Jones said. "It's the one with the bent corner."

Well, I hadn't seen it before, but sure enough, there *was* a card that had a corner a trifle bent, and when the gambler picked it up, it was the queen.

"Right!" said Leland Stanford, showing the queen around like he was delighted. "And if it doesn't have a bent corner, it might have a little speck on it, or some other such mark."

"Shit," said Price. "What's the good o' that? It don't make no difference if'n *you* know which cyard it is, do it?"

Fiddler snorted. "Feller," he said, "it's a damn good thing you're broke already."

Little Leland Stanford laughed and shuffled the cards around once again. "Where's the lady now?"

Old Comp smelled something in the wind but he didn't know what it was, so he played cautious. "Aw, shit," he said, "this'n *should* be her," and he points to the card with the bent corner.

The gambler picked it up and it was eight of clubs. "Catch on?" he said. "The idea is to let you know about the marked card, and then when the stakes get high enough, straighten it out and bend down another during the last shuffle."

"You *done* that?" said Price. "Shit."

"Watch," said Leland, and gave the cards another mix. This time all three had bent corners. Then he done it again, and all three come out like a Chinaman's shirts.

"I'll be damned," Price said. "That's a crooked game, all right."

"Only if the players are," said the gambler. "This is a game for suckers, the kind who'll only bet on a sure thing. But when they think they've got the jump on me and go the whole hog, then I give them the business."

"See, Pike," Fiddler said to Price, "it's a good thing you come in here broke, because if you hadn't, you'd of walked out of here clean as a newborn babe."

Well, everybody laughed, and old Price said, "Shit!" once more, only not in such a way as to give offense to Jones, but in a weakly in-between kind of way. Then Jones turned to the kid and said:

"Think that lucky nigger of yours could play this game to win?"

Blondie appeared to be half asleep, but straightened right up to Jones's question, like somebody had poked the right lever. "Of course, and he doesn't need any bent-up corners, either." Nothing seemed to faze the kid where that medicinal nigger was concerned.

"What do *you* think, Mr. Bradley?" said Jones. "I say the nigger hasn't a chance against the tinhorn."

"I'm with you," said Bradley, smiling in such a way it made you ashamed of saloon-keepers in general and mortified for this one in particular.

"You sure of that, now, Mr. Bradley?" Jones asked. "After you heard what Blondie said about how lucky his nigger is, leading him to all that gold and then bringing him in here to tell us about it? And you seen him find my dollar. That's a remarkable specimen of nigger, all round."

Bradley begun to look a mite uneasy, but he stuck to it, like a drowning man who feels the log he just grabbed holt of give a little sigh and thinks maybe it's an alligator but figures he'll hang on a little longer, seeing as how he hasn't got much choice.

"I'm glad of that," said Jones. "Because you're the only one here besides Blondie who's got any capital, and I think we ought to put a little something on the game, just to make it interesting. Don't you agree, Mr. Bradley?"

Well, old Bradley seen how he'd been sold, good and proper, but there wasn't no way he could get out, it being a case of die dog or eat the hatchet, so he reckoned he could spare ten dollars for the sake of a little fun.

"Ten dollars?" said Jones. "Ten horehounds!" Then he turns to the kid. "How much you willing to bet on that remarkable nigger of yours?"

"Anything," says the kid, laughing now.

Then Jones turns back to Bradley. "What's this saloon worth?"

"Hold on now," said Bradley. "Now just hold on a damned minute here. . . ."

"I reckon about a couple thousand, maybe more, maybe less," Jones said. "Blondie, Bradley and me'll match this saloon against what you took out of that mine of yours."

"Just a goddam minute," said Bradley. "What's goin' on here?"

Fiddler turned his yaller eyes around as if he only then heard Bradley squawking, like a deaf man that's been standing on a chicken.

"Why," he said, "didn't you just say you was with me?"

"Well, sure," says Bradley. "But what the hell, Jones . . . I mean, what've *you* got in the game?" He was trembling all over and sweating, like an aspen in a squall, but he stood right up there and said his piece. You had to hand it to Bradley. When his property was at stake, he *could* get his dander up.

Jones looked at him for a bit, but he didn't do more than nod once or twice. "Fair enough," he says. "Fair enough. My little purple roan is outside, and I guess everybody here knows about old Loafer. I'll put him in the pot, along with Bradley's saloon, providing Blondie throws in his mules."

"Your *horse!*" said Bradley. "Why, just the good name of this place is worth more than any damned cayuse!"

"Shut up, Mr. Bradley," said Jones. "And put up." You could tell his patience was getting thin, like the seat of a bronco-buster's trousers, and one more buck it was going to bust.

Well, Bradley tried, I'll give him credit for that. His mouth kept opening and shutting, like a frog's, and he turned pale as an old maid's ass, and just about as yaller. Dewy, he was, too, like a lemon lily at his own funeral. And quiet.

"Let's go," said Jones, looking around. "Anybody else want to get into the game?"

"Sure," said Comp Price. "Old Barnes will. He'll have a shit hem'rage if'n he's left out."

"Get him," said Jones, and Price lit out to look for Barnes. "Anybody else?" He looked over at Leland Stanford. "How about *you*, Tinhorn?"

The little gambler kept his eyes on the roof he was putting on the card house he had been building. "I'm busted," he said. "A man without a dime."

"Something tells me you're not," said Jones. "A gambler's like a ear of corn, and if you husk him down, you're more likely to find gold than red."

Leland Stanford sat there looking at his little card house, and then he give one corner a tap and it fell down. "Ever *try* to husk a gambler?"

"Now I'll tell you," said Fiddler. "I have, but never a live one."

"The same applies here," said Leland Stanford.

"That's what I figured," said Fiddler, and for a second there it looked like he was straightening hisself up at the bar for some action, but he was only scratching his back, up and then down again, up and then down.

"Right, and in which case, what happens to your game?" asked the little gambler, never once smiling.

It was Fiddler Jones who was doing all the grinning. "True enough," he said. "Course I *could* wait till after the game. Later sometime. *Any* time."

"Some corn ears are harder to find than others," said Leland Stanford. He was still mighty damn calm, but I saw him take a big swaller of nothing, and figured he was one of them kind that sweats inside. He picked up the cards and started shuffling them and I knowed it was to keep his hands busy, nothing fancy, just plain shuffling.

"Tinhorn," said Fiddler, "there ain't no advantage for either of us to carry on like this. But if you didn't have some chink in a belt under that vest of yours, I'd be mighty surprised. Yes, I would. Now Blondie here and me and Bradley has got big stakes riding on the game, and I'd just as soon you had something in it too."

The gambler stopped shuffling the cards, but his eyes stayed where they was. "I'm not saying I've got any tin on me, because maybe I have, maybe I haven't. And if I have, maybe it isn't mine to spend. But I've already told you that three-card monte is a game for fools and sharpers. Now, I'm not a fool, and I will not take lightly any imputation that I'm the other. I heard you ask the boy if his nigger would play, but I haven't heard anybody extend an invitation to me, and the plain fact is, it wouldn't do any good. I don't wish to play."

"Don't you?" said Jones. He turned back to the kid. "Blondie, supposing Tinhorn over here had something like ten gold eagles sewn in a little belt round his middle, would you match your old claim against it?"

The kid laughed. "I'll even draw him a map."

"How about it, Tinhorn. The kid here will bet his claim against whatever you got wrapped round your tummy, even if it's only your underwear. Ain't that right, Blondie."

"So long as Ham is choosing the card," the kid said.

"That's what we're talking about, ain't it?"

Well, old Leland give a little shrug. "Suit yourself," he said, picking up the cards again. "It isn't my game, but I can't turn down stakes like those."

"Get your nigger," Jones said to the kid, and then he turned to Bradley. "Seeing how we been doing pretty good by you today, how about drinks on the house for everybody in the game?"

"Yeah," said Bradley, still looking mostly like a sick frog. "On the house. While it's still here, you mean." But he took the bottle and poured Jones and the gambler a drink, and then took one for hisself. Without bothering to wet a glass.

Well, we all drunk down what we had left, those that had it, figuring we deserved it after all that talk, but when the kid come back leading that African, we wished we had held a little in reserve. Back in '78 there was one of them eclipses, in June or July it was, and it turned the whole Territory damn near black as night, like a regular twilight it was, and you could see the stars. Everybody got jumpy and uneasy, and the cows begun to bawl as if there was wolves about. Heavy, it was, like before a tornado, and you begun to breathe hard and sweat. Well, that's something like it was when that African come back into the doggery, sullen and mean-looking, and dragging his feet like they was cased in lead instead of leather.

But he come, following the kid, and stood there while Leland Stanford showed him how the game went, using just picture cards this time, and all different, so as to make it easy. The winning card was the king of spades.

"I'll give him two free tries," said the gambler. "The third is for real."

"That fair?" Jones asked, and the kid laughed and nodded. "Okay," he said. "Let's go."

Leland shuffled them cards around so fast they was invisible, but Ham didn't seem at all worried. From where I was standing, I wasn't sure he was even watching them. It seemed more like he was looking down at his feet, still scowling and sore. Well, the gambler no sooner got the jack, king, and queen spread face-down when old Ham lay a finger the size of a ripe banana, and twice as black, spang on the middle card, and he was right!

A general hubbub followed, but nobody in the game said a word. Old Leland just frowned a little and run the cards around, faster than ever, if that was possible, and Ham chose again, and it was the king, like before.

The kid begun to dance around a little, then, telling everybody to hush up for the last trick, which was for keeps, but it was a waste of breath, because nobody was saying a word by that time. Leland Stanford set the cards down and took a handkerchief out of his coat pocket to wipe his hands and forehead.

"It isn't natural," he said. "There isn't a natural man can pick them that way every time."

"Play 'em," Jones growled. He had took a cigar from Bradley's pocket and was chawing on one end, without having lit the other. It was almost like he was in a hurry to lose that horse of his.

The gambler put away his handkerchief and begun to shuffle the cards about again, but he kept on grumbling about how it was mighty fishy the nigger could get two out of two when the odds was two to one against him. He said if Ham got it a third time he was going to rewrite the law of averages. When he got done grumbling, he spread the cards wide again, one, two, three, and then took out his handkerchief for a general mop-up, and so did Bradley.

Ham stood there looking down at the cards but didn't move a finger. Instead he rolled his eyes up easy to the gambler's face and rested them there for a while, then back down to the cards again. Finally he reached out very slow, as if it was something dead laying there, and turned over the first card, which was the jack of diamonds.

"Keno!" cried out two or three, and there was a considerable uproar, but above it all you could hear Bradley screeching, "Pay up! Pay up!" He had holt of the kid and was pulling and pushing so hard that blond hair was flying every which way. "Pay up, you little son-of-a-bitch!" The kid hung limp as a rag, arms swinging and head bobbling like a drunken man's.

Leland Stanford reached out to pick up the cards with a little smile, only the nigger stopped him with one big hand, while with the other he turned over the cards that was still down. Up come the queen, but the third card wasn't the king of spades at all. It was the joker.

"A cheat!" Willie Rogers shouted out, jumping up like he had a red-hot penny down his back. "The cocksucker palmed the king!"

Leland Stanford had jumped up, too, kicking over his chair and yanking a little toy pistol out of somewheres. It was very quiet in the room just then, and you could hear the gambler plain even though his throat was full of sweat.

"It's witchcraft," he said. "There isn't no other explaining it. That black man is a witch or he's got some kind of voodoo working for him. There are people like that in New Orleans, and he's one of them. I know! That's why I palmed the card, to find out for sure, and I was right!"

"That so?" asked Jones, who hadn't ever moved from the bar. "It wasn't because you was afraid of losing whatever it is you got sewed under your vest, was it?"

The gambler begun a sneer but it didn't get very far, because like the rest of us he seen Fiddler Jones had got the drop on him with his old Colt .45.

"Put your snuffbox down, Tinhorn," he said, "before I ram it down your throat."

Well, Leland Stanford set his little noise tool on the table, but that wasn't enough for Jones, who said "Slide it," so the gambler slid it, and Willie Rogers took it up and tossed it to Fiddler, who put it away in his shirt pocket. "Take out his handkerchief," he said to Willie. "It's in his right coat pocket."

Willie done what he was told, and the missing king come tumbling out. The nigger didn't pay it no heed, but was pushing his way over to where the kid was still being held up by old Bradley, who was doing his bullfrog imitation again. You could almost hear the shit running down his legs. It wasn't so much that he hadn't won, it was more like he wasn't sure yet whether he had lost. The nigger took Blondie away from him without any trouble and went on over to the bar where he half filled a glass with whiskey for his friend. Then he upended the bottle and you could see the bubbles rising.

Nobody but me and Bradley seen all this, because the rest of the room had their eyes on Leland Stanford and Jones, and the look on the gambler's face was worth the price of admission all by itself. You could tell he wished he was somewheres else, it didn't much matter where, for the blind end of a baggage car in February was warm comfort compared to what he was staring down just then. Forty-five calibers at that range looks like a mine shaft, and you can hear the little pebbles under your feet crumbling and rattling away down in for what seems like an age. The gambler kept swallering and swallering and swallering, his Adam's apple jumping about like it wanted to leap clean out of his throat and hop right on out of that saloon.

Fiddler Jones looked at the gambler a bit, contemplating him as you might say, smiling all the while. Then he begun to lift his free hand, so slow you'd of thought there was a rattler wound around the cone of his Mexican hat which he was planning to unwind without disturbing its nap, but instead he snatched off the sombrero and let go a regular war-whoop.

"Yahoo!" he shouted out. "Yeeeah-hooo!" It was a Rebel yell, with old Jeff Davis's mint-mark all over it, the kind Texas cowboys use to get a herd moving which is unhappy about leaving a water-hole.

Well, Leland Stanford jumped like he had been goosed with a hot poker, and then he jumped again when Jones fired his .45 into the ceiling. There come a horrible scream from upstairs, and I thought for a minute Jones had done in Mrs. Bradley, but then she begun to cuss and carry on, so it appeared he hadn't, that being her normal style of conversation.

"Now, fellers," said Jones, "we're going to have a little husking bee, and find out whether this ear of corn is gold or red. If it's gold, you get to keep it, but if it's red, you can claim a kiss from me."

The little gambler put up a good fight, but those cowpunchers was so sure he had some money wrapped around him somewheres they tore the clothes right off him like wrappings off a Christmas present, only that's all there was, just the wrappings. During the ruckus the nigger and the kid tried to slip out, but Jones wouldn't let them past where he was standing. "Hold on," he said, aiming his .45 in their direction. "The fun's just started."

When the boys had got down to the gambler they was considerable upset. Nobody took Jones up on the consolation prize, and a couple of them was ready to keep right on tearing, but Jones made everybody stand back and leave the gambler alone. Even with his clothes Leland Stanford wasn't much of a man, and without them he looked like a shaved cat. He was a sorry sight and you felt ashamed for him, laying there on the floor and blinking up at that .45 Colt, waiting for what he hoped wasn't going to happen, his pecker shrunk nearly out of sight.

"Fellers," said Jones, "I'm surprised at you. Don't you know it ain't polite to leave trash lying on somebody's floor?"

So they picked him up, and when they did a funny thing happened. That king of spades was under him and stuck to his ass until he was straight up and down, and then it sort of sprung loose and fell back onto the floor. It was a simple thing, but you had to laugh, and everybody did except Leland Stanford, who stood there shivering and looking unhappy on account of he thought they was laughing at the sad spectacle he made without no clothes on.

"Well, Tinhorn," said Jones, when the laughter stopped. "You look cold. What you need is a little exercise."

"G-g-go t-to hell," said the gambler. You had to admit he had plenty of sand in him. Some little fellers is that way, you know.

KA-POW! went Jones's .45, and the king of spades did a little flip-flop, the gambler hopping right along with him. KA-POW! a little closer this time, and the dancing got livelier.

"That's the idea," said Jones. "Keep it up, Tinhorn!"

KA-POW! went the .45, and the splinters flew, and so did the gambler's bare feet.

"Everybody keep time," said Jones. "Let's help him warm up."

KA-POW! and everybody begun to whoop and holler, clapping hands, pounding tables, clinking glasses, and working up a regular shivaree. In the middle of it all, Jones jammed his big hat down over his ears and took a standing jump over the card table like a jackrabbit, grabbed up Leland Stanford and begun to whirl him around in a reel, holding him so tight his feet hardly touched the ground. The gambler tried to pry hisself loose, but he didn't have no more chance of doing so than a yearling caught by a grizzly bear. Round and round they went, everybody laughing and whooping and pounding and shóoting off guns and tossing glasses and furniture at each other, a couple fellers joining in with a buck-and-wing, hats in the air and vests and bandanas and a chair or two. It was splendid, and everybody was having a good time except Bradley. And Leland Stanford, of course. And Blondie and the nigger, who kept trying to slip out, only Jones would keep waltzing their way and block the door.

Well, Jones danced Leland Stanford around so fast that the gambler lost all his fight, and give up trying to break away or even keep his toes on the floor. Pretty soon he was in the air, and then Jones swung him even faster, around and around, so his legs and all went straight out, and then Fiddler let him go. Right through the doors he went, and on out over the board-walk, just as old Barnes and Comp Price come puffing up, Barnes lugging his old Mexican saddle with what he said was silver mountings he would always try to get in a game with if people wouldn't take his marker. Price said the gambler simply scaled across the street like a flat stone, slapping the mud once or twice before he finally landed on the far side.

"Whut in the name o' pink carnations wuz thet?" asked Barnes.

"Shit, Barnes," said Price, or so he told us later. "Thet wuz yer game."

We all come tumbling out then to take a look, but for a minute or so there wasn't nothing to see. Then way over on the other side of the street there was a kind of bubble rose up out of the red muck which turned into a lump, and out of that lump there come arms and legs. It was Adam and the Creation all over again.

Then out of that lump there come a mouth, and out of that mouth there come puffs of steam and amazing words, nothing like Adam would ever of thought to use. It wasn't we was just buggers, oh, no! And we wasn't mere sons-a-bitches, neither. That wasn't gaudy enough for the likes of us. And bastards! Why, he had us being the illegitimate litter of every strange and wonderful creature in the zoo, all the time shaking his fist and backing up out of that slew onto the other boardwalk. It *was* amazing, a regular entertainment, and educational, too.

I had always heard tell that travel broadens a man, and judging from that little gambler's range, he had spread hisself considerable since leaving home. Why, it was a college degree just to stand there and listen, and we would of paid admission for a repeat performance. When he had run through his repertoire, we all cheered and clapped for a encore, but he just shook his muddy fist at us some more and then slopped away down the boardwalk until he could slip between two buildings and disappear, for all the world like a shit storm on legs.

When we got back inside Bradley was just finishing up with his broom, and the kid and the nigger was over at the bar where we had left them. So was Jones, and so was his Colt .45. Blondie was crying, or had been crying, but anyways was clinging to that African, who was making little noises with his lips and stroking the kid's long blond hair.

"Jesus Christ," somebody said. "What's *this* proposition?"

"Make a nice pair, don't they," said Bradley, giving a last push to his little pile of trash. "Ought to be cast in plaster and put on somebody's mantel."

Jones was standing there looking at the kid and the nigger, sawing away at his shoulder with the .45. Then he reached up and tipped the sombrero back off his head, which was held by a braid of rawhide so it could lay on his shoulders behind, Mexican style.

"She's been scared, fellers," he said. "She needs some cheering up."

With that, Jones begun to stomp a rhythm with his boot and give the sign for everybody to do the same, which they done, clapping and hopping around the room, some with partners, and the shivaree started in all over again, the bottles and glassware on the shelfs shaking and clinking and one or two things falling to the floor with a smash.

"Hold on there!" said Bradley, only without much hope. "Ain't you done enough damage for one day?"

Jones was hopping around all by hisself, doing a wild kind of fandango, which was mostly polka, with a shuffle-and-breakdown added, whirling and twirling, his Mexican hat flopping like a big bird hanging onto his neck, and the medals on it chinking and clinking along with his spurs. He was shouting and whooping, like he didn't have a care in the world, and give Bradley's little pile of plaster and glass a kick, so most of it somehow landed on Bradley, and then went whirling away, only always keeping hisself between the door and the nigger and the kid.

The nigger kept trying to leave, all the same, and you could tell that all the noise and confusion was making him nervous. He had holt of Blondie, who was white and limp as any sheet, and he kept dodging this way and that so as to keep out of people's way and not make no trouble, his eyes jittery and his skin that ashy color which a scared nigger will get. He was making some progress, and was halfway to the door when Fiddler give a great leap and landed right in front of them, his boots planted apart and his elbows out, for all the world like a six-foot-tall fighting rooster.

"A-roo-a-roo-aroooo!" he crowed, flapping his arms, his yaller eyes blazing like headlamps. "Here's a cock for a chicken! A-roo-a-roo-arooooo!" Then he reached out to grab Blondie away from the nigger.

When I was in the War they had a big Parrott gun hid out in the swamps on James Island, which they was using to pound the shit out of Charleston. It was a big bastard, and black, and ugly, and when it went off you could hear the sound for miles, a kind of *thump*! which you could feel in your back molars. When the nigger's fist let go that old Parrott gun come direct to mind, almost as fast as it went to Fiddler's forehead, and there was the exact same *thump*. The nigger caught him right between the eyes, and dropped him like some steer in a slaughterhouse, only it was more like the pictures I seen once in a scientific book of a mule they had wired up to ten cameras and some dynamite, so as to see what it looked like coming to pieces when the charge went off.

First you seen the old mule just standing there, as only a mule can stand, with its head down and half asleep, and in the next picture it was a little shaky-looking, but still a mule, and in the next picture it begun to come apart, but you could still see it was a mule, and in the next it looked a little less like a mule, and so on until there wasn't nothing but a big ball of fuzzy stuff. In the last picture all there was left was the mule's head, still hanging in the air, right where it had been from the start, only the eyes was wide open now instead of being almost closed. The book never did say what that mule had done to deserve it, but it must of been atrocious.

Well, that's what come to mind after Fiddler Jones got hit between the eyes by the nigger's fist. He just seemed to bust apart, bit by bit, and what started out Fiddler Jones ended up a soft pile of mush on Bradley's floor. I'll never forget them yaller eyes, staring up out of the pile. Wide open, they was, like the mule's, and shining yet. Even today when I hear the word "surprise," that's what I think of, them yaller, staring eyes of Fiddler Jones, departed. Because he *was* dead, and you didn't need no coroner's jury to tell you how.

It was funny, but for a few seconds nobody in that place stirred except old Bradley. The shivaree had stopped when Jones let out his last whoop, and after the nigger struck him down everybody just stood where they was, like kids playing statue. But Bradley, who had got behind his bar to keep from getting stepped on, he reached down underneath for his sawed-off scattergun, and then sort of rolled over the bar and come down on his feet with the gun on the nigger. Very fast it was, and smooth, for a fat man like Bradley.

"Okay," he said. "Okay, now. I knew there'd be trouble when this nigger showed up, and I was right. Now are you boys going to let this black bastard walk out of here, scot free, with a white man laying dead on the floor?"

Well, it was a gilt-edge invitation, and the fellers accepted it right off. The nigger tried to make it to the door, dragging Blondie along, but the whole saloon dropped on him, like the ceiling, you might say, and drug him down and held him. It took a bit of doing, naturally, and in the tussle the kid got flung to one side like a rag tossed by a bull, and lay in a heap, bawling like a baby. Everybody put their attention to the nigger, who was straining hard to get loose, the big veins in his neck and head swelling like grapevines on a tree trunk, shiny and black after it has rained, and every now and then he would get a fist loose and do some damage before two or three men got it held down again. For a while there wasn't much talk, just a deal of groaning and grunting and cussing and moaning, but once they got him pinned down and hog-tied with two or three criss-crossed lariats, old Bradley made a little speech.

"Good work, men," he said, walking over and giving the nigger a jab with his scattergun. "Now let's take him outside and finish the job. All we need is a knife and some coal oil."

Well, I seen it was time for me to do my little act, so I give Bradley a small tap behind the ear with my gun butt and he dropped very quiet to the floor, right alongside the late Fiddler Jones.

"All right, now," I said. "If we're going to hang this nigger, we're going to hang him legal."

"Aw-you-lousy-shit-face," said Comp Price, still panting and puffing down on the floor. "Ever-body-seen-it."

"That's right," I said. "I seen it too. I seen a lot of things today, as a matter of fact, but there's one thing I ain't going to see, and that's a lynching. You got witnesses enough, all you aching to see the nigger hung, so there shouldn't be no problem in getting your wish, so long as I get mine."

"Aw, you tin-badge bastards make me sick," said Price, beginning to get his breath back. "Why can't we have a little fun?"

"Why, that's all you been having, Comp," I said. "Ain't it about time you begun sharing your fun with the rest of our town? They won't take it lightly if you don't."

"Aw," he said, and the other cowboys grumbled some too, but in the end they done what I said to do, since I had the gun.

"Come on," said Willie Rogers. "Let's git him down to the jail so's to get the thing over and done with afore supper."

I had them take the kid along, too, in case somebody got some unusual ideas in that direction, and when we finally got them safe into the jailhouse, there was the Captain sitting in his office, cleaning out a pipe with his penknife, the stem clenched under his stump arm like in a vise.

"Hello, boys," he said. "What took you so long?" He folded up the penknife and took down his ring of keys. "I've been expecting you for an hour."

"The nigger killed Fiddler Jones," I said.

"Is that right? Then there's bound to be a good deal of weeping and wailing throughout the Territory." He come out of his office and run his eye over the crowd. "Guess we better lock 'em both up," he said, leading the way back to the calaboose.

That left me to entertain the rest of the party. There was quite a few had crowded into the jailhouse with something in mind, they wasn't sure what, and considerable more with similar inclinations was gathering outside, the news having spread. Lafe Chancellor come pushing his way in, having seen the crowd from his store across the street, and found out what was going on.

"Gonna be a hangin', looks like," he announced to nobody in particular. "I'm gonna need some help buildin' the scaffold."

"Scaffold, shit!" said Price. "All we need's a overhead beam and a box."

"Goddam it, Price," said Lafe, getting a trifle red around the neck. "It's right there in my contract with the town. This ain't no damn mining camp, don't forgit, but a reg'lar town, and I got a reg'lar contract for the gallows on low bid, all legal-like."

"*Only* bid, don't ya mean?" Price said, which was true enough. "Damn waste o' money, if'n you ast me."

"Which nobody did, Price," said the Captain, coming back with his keys. "Now you and Lafe and the rest clear out of here. There isn't going to be any hanging. . . ."

"NO HANGING!" cried out a half dozen, and Price put on a smug look and nodded to everybody around him as if to say he had told us so.

"Hold on!" the Captain shouted. "I meant no hanging before a judgment, for God's sake!"

"Well, let's git on with it, then," said Price. "No sense wasting more o' the taxpayers' money."

"C'mon, now," I said, beginning to push them back a little, only not too hard. "Let's get moving."

"When's the trial gonna be?" asked Price, pushing the other way. "That's what I want ter know."

"Soon as I get the Judge," said the Captain.

"C'mon, boys," said Price, "let's git up thar and git seats afore the whole damn town shows up."

"Hold on," said Lafe, as they begun to push past him. "I'll give a quarter to any man who'll pitch in and help me with the scaffold." He held up a paper roll and waved it.

"Ya know whut ya kin do with yer damn quarter, Chancellor," said Price. "And that goes fer the hull roll, too."

"Half dollar, then."

"Fuck the half dollar. I ain't worried where we're gonna hang 'im, but I want ter make damn sure he gits jedged good an' proper. Fust things fust, I allus say."

Well, there was a general scramble out of there, and you could hear their boots on the outside stairs leading up to the room where the Judge done his presiding, then there come a dreadful rumble and screaking of chairs and benches.

"Ain't nobody goin' to give me a hand?" said Lafe. "Fine town this is. How we goin' to have a proper legàl hangin' without no scaffold?"

"Don't worry about it, Chancellor," said the Captain. "If you want to build your scaffold on spec, you'll find plenty of help from the leftovers outside."

"On spec?" Chancellor said. "Christ almighty, Cap'n, how many witnesses to a murder do you need?"

"Until the Judge has had his say, that man back there is as innocent as you are, Chancellor."

"You talking 'bout that nigger, Cap'n?"

"I'm talking about the accused, Chancellor. Now you move on out of here. . . ."

"Ain't nobody lines Lafe Chancellor up with no nigger, I don't care what he's got pinned to his vest."

"Aw, Lafe," I said, "the Captain wasn't comparing you to nobody. He just wants you out of here, so we can get ready for the trial. And if you want to get that gallows built, you better hustle along."

"That's right, Chancellor," said the Captain.

"All of it?"

"As much of it as you want."

"Well, I accept your apology, Cap'n, only you ought to be more careful. Law-abidin' citizens don't take kindly to bein' lined up with murderin' niggers."

"Well, Winky," said the Captain, as soon as Lafe had gone grumbling out, "there goes your General Good to pick out some crooked three-by-fours and some knotty planking to charge up to town expense."

"Aw, Lafe don't mean no harm," I said.

"That's right," he said. "Nobody ever means any harm." He had got that poetry look, so I changed the subject quick.

"Want me to go shake out the Judge?"

"No, you stay here and keep an eye on what's locked up out back." He went on up the stairs, and I went back to the calaboose, and there they was, the nigger still hog-tied, and lying on a bunk, and the kid in there with him, trying to work the knots loose.

"Here," I said, reaching for my knife, but then the kid looked up at me and I thought better of it. "Never mind," I said, "only you'd have better luck if the nigger'd stop trying to bust them ropes."

The kid never said a word, only went back to working at the knots, scrabbling away like some kind of little animal with hands and teeth and making whiny noises. I stayed there to watch as long as I could, which wasn't more than a minute or so, and then went back up to the Captain's office. There was something mighty strange about that pair, and it wasn't just the madness or the deaf-and-dumbness or the nigger's medicinal properties. It come to me that maybe what Fiddler Jones had been saying about sheepmen and their ways had some truth in it, and if it did then it would be a mercy to put a bullet in the blond head and another in the black one, and not to dignify what they was with any trial. Somehow they seemed worse than murder, and could only bring the town more shame than ever, and maybe even the kind of doom which would make the long winter we had just gone through seem a treat.

V

The Judge had shipped considerable whiskey since breakfast, but other than that he seemed in pretty fair shape, and come stumbling down behind the Captain, sighing and moaning under his breath like he always done, being so grass-bellied and all.

"Now, Captain," he was saying, "you're sure this ain't *my* nigger? You wouldn't lie to me about such a thing, would you?"

"Take a look for yourself, Judge," the Captain said. "They're locked up back there, both of them."

The Judge stood there, weaving back and forth and holding onto the wall. He didn't have many teeth left, and wouldn't take the Captain's advice about getting new ones, so he was chewing on his gums, the white bristles on his face moving about like porcupine quills.

"*Both* on 'em?" he said. "The nigger didn't come alone?"

"There's a boy, too," the Captain said, though you could see it didn't make him none too happy to say it.

The Judge looked at him and then at me, rolling his eyes

hard over without moving his head, like a bulldog will, and they was bulldog eyes, too, all bloodshot and muddy where the chalky blue give off to white.

"Hold on now," he said. "You didn't say nothing upstairs about a boy being mixed up in this."

"That's right," said the Captain. "But it'll come out in the trial."

"Whut's the boy look like?"

"Help yourself, Judge. He's in there with the nigger."

"Whut's his name?"

"He never said."

Well, the Judge heaved a deep sigh and shoved off from the wall towards the lockup, rocking this way and that and every so often reaching out for the wall as he went.

"He thinks maybe the boy is his friend, too, don't he?" I said.

"I don't know what he thinks," said the Captain. "But that's as good a guess as any."

" 'A boy and a nigger, a nigger and a boy,' that's what he told us to watch for, Captain."

"That's right," said the Captain.

The Judge didn't stay back there long, but come weaving up to the office, blinking and staring at the floor as he come.

"Cap'n," he said. "Somebody ought to untie that poor nigger. Those knots is tied awful cruel."

"We'll have to put irons on him, then, Judge. He's a violent man."

The Judge looked at us and give a little shudder and a moan. "Well," he said, "irons is awful too, but anything is better than bein' hog-tied like some animal, I reckon." He didn't say nothing more, just shuffled on past and on up the stairs to get ready for the trial, which meant putting on his hat.

"I guess he's satisfied," I said. "I guess he knows that these ain't his friends."

"We're going to need some help, Winky," said the Captain.

"Run upstairs and cut out a couple of sober ones and deputize them."

Well, I stepped out of the office and there was Matt Pringle and Tom Gardiner standing in the doorway, peering in, so I took them back to the Captain and he swore them, and pinned badges on them, and then all four of us went back to the calaboose with irons and a padlock. It was a hell of a lot easier than we expected, on account of the nigger just lay there while we cut the lariat ropes and didn't budge till the irons was on him. The kid cried some more, or a little harder, since the blubbering hadn't never really stopped, but didn't try to get in our way. It did seem like they knowed they had come to the end of something.

Then we went back to the office and the Captain told Tom and Matt what their duties was, which was to guard the nigger and the kid while the trial was going on.

"Huh!" said Tom. "They 'pear more like they need a nurse than a guard."

"It ain't them you got to watch," I said. "It's the others."

"That's right," said the Captain. "Jones has got more friends in this town now that he's dead than he ever had when he was alive."

"I don't much like it," said Matt. "Riding herd on a nigger, and maybe havin' to shoot one of yer pards to save his stinkin' black hide."

"You won't have to do any shooting," said the Captain. "All I want you to do is sit there, both of you, and keep your badges and scatterguns in plain view. If any trouble starts, Winky and I can take care of it."

We went upstairs, the Captain leading, then the nigger and the kid, then Matt and Tom, with me covering from the rear. When we traipsed past his room, I seen the Judge sitting in his chair and looking out the window, like always, so it did look as though he had got *his* nigger separated from ours. The courtroom was jam-packed with people, most of them the same gang

as was in Bradley's doggery, including Bradley hisself, who had
got rigged up in a big gauze bandage and looked for all the
world like the mad Turk in the play. He still had that froggy
air, and the dirty look he threw me didn't have much pepper
behind it. I guess he figured he was lucky to be where he was in
the shape he was in, and still have a place to go back to when it
was all over.

The place was stuffed full of cowboys, like I said, and the air
was full of smoke and smells of horseshit, cowshit, sweat, beer,
and whiskey, and had that other flavor too, the one you get if
you throw open a hamper full of dirty old clothes and stick
your beezer down into it. That was a gamy bunch, all round,
and itching for some action that they could help along. When
we come into the room, everybody begun to shout at once,
wanting to be witnesses, and you would of thought we was
getting up a filibustering party instead of a trial. It did look like
Jones had growed more friends than his ass had pimples.

The Captain quick picked out a half-dozen of the soberest,
and told everybody else they would have to keep their mouths
shut or get out, that there was a crowd of folks outside which
would be glad to have their seats if *they* didn't want them,
because of course they did. Well, the boys was very good-
natured the whole time, but I noticed nobody looking over at
the kid and the nigger, which was sitting to one side with Matt
and Tom inside a little corral we had there for the accused.

Then the Captain went out and got the Judge, and he come
in and sat down and rapped with his mallet for order and si-
lence and got it straight off. That bunch hadn't come but for
one thing, and they knowed the quieter they was the quicker it
would come, and through the windows in front you could hear
the hammering and sawing where Chancellor had got some
boys to help him put the scaffold together after all.

Well, I was the first witness swore, and told all I had to tell,
and then the others come up, and told it all over again, pretty
much the same, only they kept cutting it shorter and shorter

till the last witness, which was Willie Rogers, just said, "It was like they already told you, Judge." The whole time they was talking, I seen how the Judge couldn't keep from staring at Blondie and the nigger, looking first at the one, then at the other. His little blue eyes didn't have that far-away look in them any more, and they didn't have that patient, doggy look, neither.

That was his way, to study everybody who come up before him. He was a great believer in faces, and held that they was more important than any other kinds of evidence. But I never seen him look so hard or so long as he looked at that crazy kid and the nigger. It was like he was trying to figure out more than just whether the nigger was guilty or not. It was more like he was trying to understand what they was, the two of them, not just then and there, but away back at the beginning, long before they come to Besterman. It was more like the both of them was on trial, not just the nigger. Because after Willie stepped down, looking a trifle ornery on account of nobody left him nothing to witness, the Judge turned to them both and asked if they had anything to say.

It was the Captain had to remind the Judge that the nigger was deaf and dumb, and so the Judge asked the kid to speak for the nigger, in his place, as you might say. The kid looked up for the first time since they was brung into the room, and was purely scared, I reckon, pale right to the lips, which was bluish, like watered milk, and bluish around the eyes, too. I remembered then that neither of them had slept for days, and I couldn't help feeling sorry for that set of poor locoes, the nigger who was about to get hung and his friend, who wasn't.

"He didn't mean to do anything wrong," the kid said, in that funny little preacher's voice. "It wasn't his fault, your Honor. He wanted us to get out of town, that's all. He told me that the man was going to make trouble for us, but I told him. . . ." Blondie's voice caught back for a split second, stumbled as you might say, and you could see the salt water welling up inside once more, but the slosh was kept back this time. "I told him he could go if he wanted. I told him I would catch up to him later, but he wouldn't leave without me. And that . . . that man and the gambler got hold of me, and Ham didn't have anything to do with that, either. But I told him we couldn't lose because of his powers. I . . . I . . . ."

Well, the pumps begun to work again, and Blondie started in snuffling and carrying on so the words couldn't wade through the water. Even knowing all I knowed, I got a big lump in my throat and when I looked around the room I seen there wasn't a man in there who wasn't leaning forward and waiting for the kid to finish telling their side of the story, and some was blinking hard and swallowing hard, too. You see, cowboys is a terrible sentimental bunch, especially when they are liquored up, and these punchers had taken on quite a cargo. A cowboy is always on a rampage when he isn't working, either fighting, or laughing, or screwing, or crying, and sometimes he'll do all four at once.

Now they didn't know no better, but I did. I didn't have no excuse to feel sorry for that kid. Damn it all, I said to myself. You know what happened in that saloon. You know what the Captain said about this kid and the nigger, that they ain't no better than miners and cannibals, loony through and through. And you seen what you saw downstairs in the calaboose, and would of plugged both of them then and there if somebody had asked you to. What's wrong with you?

Well, I swallowed a couple times, but the lump stayed right where it was. I looked over at the Captain, who was sitting at a table to one side of the Judge, where he wrote into a ledger all that went on during a trial. He kept all the ledgers on a shelf down in his office, and I asked him why one time.

"Just in case," he said.

"In case what?" I said.

"Well, if this town burns down or blows away," he said, "maybe these books will survive so it won't have all been in vain."

I peeked into one of them and it was all in squiggly little marks, a code the Captain had learned before the War when he had been a newspaper reporter. So what the hell good was it going to be to anybody but him? And he never looked into them ledgers once they was on the shelf. So it did seem like a whole lot of damn foolishness, and a considerable waste of time.

Anyhow, the Captain had stopped writing into his ledger and was looking over at the kid, and there wasn't no blinking or water about *his* eyes, nor was he swallowing, only just squinting a bit, with his jaw pulled in the way he always done when things took a turn he hadn't figured on. Then I seen his eyes move to the other side of the room, and when I turned to find out why, there was the little gambler standing up waiting for the Judge to see him.

I'll be damned if I know how he got in there. I know he wasn't in the room when the trial started, but he was now, and was all bugged up in a new suit with a smart vest and watch chain, with a Masonic fob hanging from it. How all that got through the people outside, which was crowded up the stairs and on the platform, and through the door, and into a room packed as tight as bullets in a box, I never found out, but there he was. And he didn't look like a gambler no more, but damn near respectable, no worse than a sharp drummer or a lawyer or a candidate for senator.

"Your Honor," he says, finally, because like most everybody in the room, the Judge hadn't took his eyes off the kid and the nigger, "your Honor, may I speak?"

Well, the Judge turned to look at him, but he seemed a trifle peeved at having his mood broke into. "Who's this?" he said.

Up I popped, eager as a pup and as damned foolish: "That's Leland Stanford, Judge!" I said, without thinking, and there was a big horse-laugh went round. It wasn't all that funny I didn't think.

The little gambler just stood there smiling until everybody had died down, and then he says he appreciates the compliment, but he was the humble bearer of a less well-known name in the annals of the West, and give it out like a card on a silver platter, Something Sturgis or Sturgis Something, I never could remember.

"But," he said, "that is of no importance," with a little wave of his hand as if he was tossing his own card into a wastebasket, so you knew who he was didn't make no difference, only what he was about to say. Oh, he was slick and smooth, that Sturgis, for all the world like the barrel of a gun that's just come out of its crate.

"You will recall," he begun, "that during the testimony of the several witnesses, some casual mention was made of a . . . shall we say ludicrous incident involving the late Jones and myself. . . ."

"Ludercriss?" old Price shouted out. "Shit, feller, it were hilarious!"

Well, a few jackasses had their bray, and the Judge thumped them down, but the most of us was wondering what card the little gambler had up his sleeve this time, standing up like he was and speechifying in such a regular court-roomy way. Not that it surprised me all that much. I give odds that old Sturgis had been around enough courtrooms for the lingo to stick to him, like dandruff to a comb. Still, it *was* impressive, like Roman candles when all that had been advertised was Chinese crackers.

"Since I was involved in that humorous episode, which seems to have directly preceded and may have precipitated the incident which is the main concern of this trial, perhaps my testimony is of some value here."

The Judge looked over at the Captain, who was still staring at the gambler, this being the first time he had set eyes on him, and he still had that jaw drawed back in, which meant he hadn't come to no conclusions yet, so the Judge was on his own.

"Keep it plain," he said.

"Your Honor," said the gambler, "I should like to point out extenuating circumstances. The man who was killed today by a blow of the fist meant solely to dissuade him from an intended ignominy, if not an assault, was a scoundrel of the deepest dye, a thief and a murderer who had the respect of cowards and weaklings only. A man who kept decent citizens at bay through threats of violence and death. A man—I dislike that word in the present context—a beast who constantly menaced the peace of this community. Can anyone deny it?" Sturgis folded his arms and took a regular Fourth-of-July stand, with one foot half a pace in front of the other, and held it for damn near a full second, for all the world like a man riding a mustang around a corral that he has just broken in. You could tell he knew he was in charge, that those ten-dollar and twenty-dollar words was being plucked out of the air by them cowboys as though they was real money. "No one denies it," he said, with a quiet little smile, and then puffing his cheeks full of new, shiny words that would come spilling out just as easy as if he owned the mint.

"Although I was not present when the fatal blow was struck . . ."

"You sure's hell wasn't," said Price, loud and clear, and there was a few guffaws, but not so many as before, and the rest of the people shushed them quiet. Because that little gambler had *style*, a fool could see that, and if there's one thing a cowboy admires, it's style.

"Though I was not present, as I say, yet the witnesses have testified as to the violence intended to the person and, more important, to the self-respect and dignity of the friend of the accused. This boy . . . nay, I say *child*, for his guileless face still shines with the innocence imbibed at his mother's breast, this child was unable had he the means to defend himself from the vile actions of his calumniator. Instead, his friend, his partner, and his adopted brother, this humble and afflicted African, was inspired by the inmost urgings of his simple heart to do what the least of us would have done had we been in his place. Your Honor, the blow struck was struck in the name of friendship and decency, those twin virtues, those sacred Gemini without which no human community can long endure. Your Honor, I contend that this honorable Court, pledged as it is to the affirmation of law and order and to the preservation of the community, must find the accused innocent of any wrongdoing."

Sturgis sat down then, but everybody else stood up, hollering and stomping and clapping and tossing their hats in the air. You couldn't tell for sure if they agreed with him or not, but nobody in that room could keep from giving the little gambler his due for that gaudy, gilt-edge, engraved-on-steel certificate-of-merit which he had just drawed up for the nigger and right out of his own head, too. Then, outside through the window, you could see people looking up from where they was working on the gallows, and they begun to whoop and holler also, thinking the verdict was give and the nigger was meat ripe for hanging.

The Judge didn't pound down the commotion. He just sat there looking at Sturgis, like he was still trying to figure out what half them words was all about. Then I seen that the Captain had got up and come around so he was standing in front of his little desk. You could tell that things wasn't going to his liking, because his jaw wasn't drawed back in any more, but stuck forward, and I knowed he was about to set that trial on the right tracks. Everybody else seen him up there too, and pretty soon the room was almost quiet again so as to find out what the Captain had to say.

"Your Honor," he begun, "since a voice has been raised in defense of the accused, it is in the interest of justice that someone speak in the role of prosecutor. . . ."

Somebody said, "Sit down, Army," but it was behind a hat or a hand, because I never seen who done it, and the Judge banged down his mallet for quiet.

"Keep it simple, Cap'n," he said.

"Your Honor," said the Captain, "I cannot refute what this gentleman has so eloquently stated, nor do I intend to try. That the accused struck a blow in the name of friendship and decency, and that the late C. A. Jones, alias Fiddler Jones, was a known criminal, is all perfectly true. But what is also true, and equally irrefutable, is that the blow was fatal, and that it was thereby murderous, and by virtue of that an offense to the same community which our eloquent visitor apparently holds sacred."

Well, there was some grumbling and talk, but the Captain just plowed right along, only raising his voice somewhat so as to be heard.

"Your Honor," he said, "we live in constant peril, making our abode on an outpost of civilization, a frontier of unequaled savagery, where raw Nature rests like a mountain lion at the very thresholds of our homes. It is difficult to say, at any moment, when we may or may not be overwhelmed by the forces of wildness, of chaos, of lawlessness. In a more settled, more orderly community, persons like Jones would not walk free and unhampered, licensed by fear to commit mischief with impunity. We know that in other towns he did indeed murder and steal, but those acts were committed outside the bounds of our jurisdiction and are of no account here. And until the time of his death, Jones did nothing within this place, committed no felony, no larceny, nothing more than the common nuisances such as are tolerated by this community daily. Had he done otherwise, he would have been immediately apprehended and incarcerated for the well-being and peace of the town.

"What, then, was Jones struck dead for, but a malicious prank merely, an unbearable insult, perhaps, but one against which no legal stricture has been written? In short, he was guilty of no crime, and only apprehended by the accused in the commission of what may have been nothing more than a harmless gesture, not an act complete.

"The accused, we are told in moving terms, was motivated by the passion of friendship and loyalty. But it is not our duty here to define the *intention* of the act, only its consequence. Of intention we seldom can learn much. Of our own intentions we know little, of others', scarcely more than they wish us to discover. Of the consequence, however, there can be no doubt. A man is dead.

"Further, even were we to admit the most honorable intentions, such intentions are not, despite claims to the contrary, justification for murder. We have heard that the blow was struck as a deterrent only, and that the death of Jones was an accident. I submit, your Honor, that it was a blow struck in anger, and had the instrument been a knife or a gun rather than a fist, that the passion behind the act would have been none the less for the circumstance. There are fists in this world, your Honor, which are as deadly as the rifled tube.

"If each of us were permitted, your Honor, to strike blows for what we considered offended decency and outraged friendship, using whatever weapons were convenient to us at the time, I maintain that we would soon find ourselves living in chaos. We cannot all be judges unto ourselves and each other. It is for that reason we submit our wills to the common will of the community, here vested in you. And on the borders of civilization, where order is constantly threatened by the lawlessness of raw Nature, and by the lawlessness in men which raw Nature inspires, we must be particularly scrupulous in our respect for the common good.

"Without it, our community would collapse, order giving way to disorder, sane logic to insane reasoning, regard for property and the rights of others to the common exercise of greed and rapacity. Like the aboriginal inhabitants of this Territory, your Honor, we would be little better than wild animals —savage, ignorant, naked, unhoused. For such is the state of Nature, where the primitive values of friendship and decency do indeed maintain sway, but where unregulated passions bathe tooth and claw in the red ink of moral bankruptcy. Given the choice between savagery and civilization, your Honor, I for one find no difficulty in choosing the latter. Those whose sympathies are with the accused, I fear, will be choosing the former.

"But, your Honor, I doubt if many in this room sympathize with the accused. We have heard an argument built on the foundations of innocence, not the innocence of the accused, but of his friend. The innocence of the boy, however, is not the issue of this trial. To be innocent, merely, is truly the prerogative of the child, as we have been told, and we must not confuse it with the quality of innocence with which this court must deal, which is to say the absence of any complicity in the crime before the bench. The boy may be innocent in that regard, indeed he probably is, but once again, that is not the issue here. We are met to determine the innocence of the accused, and we have not heard today *one word* to that point, but only a brief catalogue of what are assumed to be extenuating circumstances, a list whose validity I categorically deny.

"A man lies dead, your Honor. It could have been any of us in this room, the accused and his friend excepted. A man lies dead, and his slayer must not go unpunished."

Well, that was it, and the Captain went around back of his table and sat down again with his ledger. There wasn't any cheering or hollering this time, but there wasn't no hissing neither. Everybody just sat there, staring, and you could tell they was trying to figure out what had happened. When they come in there, it was to get the Judge's permission to take the nigger out and hang him. Then the kid got them snuffling and doubting, and old Sturgis led them around the ring till they faced in the other direction, thinking maybe they ought to pin a medal on the nigger and shake his hand for what he done.

Next thing, here comes the Captain and gives them a dose of salts, so as to flush all that out of them, and now they was empty twice over, which is very damn clean. It did look as though we ought to hang the nigger after all, only there wasn't the seasoning for it in this stew, like there was down in the street, where the gallows was about built and the rest of the town had turned out, kids climbing up to roost on posts and their folks trying to pull them down so they could shinny up theirselves.

Well, it was so quiet in the room you could hear the Judge sigh. He sat slumped back in his chair, with his head resting deep down in his shoulders, and you could tell he was troubled. Only his old beaver plug was straight up and down, like always. The rest of him was all collapsed inside hisself. He didn't move at all, just kept his eyes on the nigger, and I knowed he was trying to feel the thing through, like a man inside a cave with his lantern out.

Then, down in the street, somebody started up a song which everybody outside joined in with, and the words come through the windows very clear, even though they was still nailed shut because of the cold.

"Let's hang that nigger to a sour-apple tree,
    Hang that nigger to a sour-apple tree. . . ."

That crowd was getting impatient, having thought some time back that the verdict was already give, so the Captain sent Matt down to tell them the trial wasn't yet over, and they should pipe down. You could hear his voice, too, shouting up from down in the street, and then all the catcalls and such, but pretty soon it was almost quiet again. Even so, it was only after Matt had got back upstairs and was just sitting down when the Judge begun to speak, and when he did it was so low at first you had to lean forward and cup your ear.

". . . a long ways," he was saying. "We come a long ways to where we get sense enough to know a nigger and a Injun is the same as a white man when it comes to fren'ship and decency, and when there's nothing betwixt a man and the world but his partner, it don't make a damn bit of diff'rence the color of his hide. And the world *is* hate and anger and murder, ain't it? Yes, and who does most of the hatin' and murderin'? The Injun and the nigger ain't got no monop'ly, and Nature's got her laws, too, only you got to learn the signs, which ain't written in no book.

"Now, Fiddler Jones was a rotten, low-down, ornery son-of-a-bitch, and yet he was a man, and white, too. They ain't hardly a man in this room wouldn't a shot him if they was in the right and could a got the drop on him, from behind a bar'l, bush, or barn. We all know that. But was the nigger in the right?

"I been a-sittin' here lookin' at this boy and his nigger, and I can see they got a powerful tie betwixt them. They come a long ways together. Now the nigger killed a man, jest the same as any one of us, like the Cap'n says, and maybe he wanted to kill him, maybe not. There just ain't no way of finding out. If Fiddler Jones had come after the nigger with a gun or knife, why that would be one thing, wouldn't it? But he went for the boy with his empty hands, which is another.

"I got to say I never heard such fine talk about fren'ship and decency in all my born days. But I don't think the little man who did all the talkin' gives a pig's fart fer fren'ship and decency. I think he's stuffed full of hate, all in a sweat to git back at a dead man for tossin' him in the muck, and maybe get just a little closer to the boy and his gold whilst he's at it. I don't even think he cares much whether or not we hang that nigger, so long as he can get next to the boy. And if we hang the nigger, we might as well hang the boy, too, for he won't last out the week.

"And I think the Cap'n done a handsome job defendin' law an' order, and that's what he gets paid to do. But law an' order hain't all there is, nor is this town nor civilization, nuther. And most of us come out here to the Territory for one of two reasons, either to get shunt of civilization or to get rich. Well, as soon as those who wanted them finds them, they wake up and find a dozen others jest arrived to take them away, which warn't theirs to take in the first place, since everything belonged to the Injuns. Well, the Injuns don't believe in property, and is glad to trade off what they don't own for a bunch of medals and such trash from the gov'ment, which takes it in the name of civilization. And that's *us*, Cap'n, us and all the people out in the street which is hankering to string up a nigger because he kilt a white man in the name of fren'ship, which nobody else had the guts to do.

"Now they ain't no doubt that the nigger here is on the side of Nature. Even the Cap'n and the gambler agrees on *that* point. But whose side was Fiddler Jones on? And whose side are *we* on?

"Well, they's got to be exceptions, Cap'n, or the world would be so damned civilized a body'd be better off dead."

Then the Judge looked around the room, and you could see the eyes falling down like grass will when a scythe takes a sweep.

"I find this nigger, Ham, not guilty," he said.

Well, for a minute there everybody sat so still you could of took their tintype, but then all hell broke loose, everybody screaming and howling and ki-yiing their lungs out. People was rushing up and pumping the Judge's hand up and down till his damned hat nearly fell off, and there was others congratulating the gambler and some the Captain—for doing the best he could, you know—and then they made them both come together to shake hands, which they done but without no real warmth to it. The Captain had his mouth pulled back so you could see his teeth, but it wasn't no smile, and Sturgis looked plumb foolish.

The kid was crying and laughing and wig-waggling to the nigger, who stood there trembling like a mustang outside the blacksmith's shop, his eyes going this way and that, the people just swarming around them, cheering and hollering, and pushing them out of the room and down the stairs, such a shoving and yelling you couldn't hold back or hear yourself think, but just went right along with the rest. The nigger was doing his damnedest to grab onto things as they come by, and you could see that he was upset and worried by all the ruckus. He was looking around in that wild way of his, trying to find where the kid was, and flailing his arms around. Every now and then somebody would get a clout on the head or arm with them chains he had on, but nobody paid them no heed.

Well, there was the crowd outside waiting, and when they see us all coming down the stairs with the nigger, they sent up another shout, and come swarming towards us, and when the people from inside got down on the boardwalk and tried to lift Ham up on their shoulders to take him back down to Bradley's, the other crowd snatched him away from them, and begun to drag him along, everybody cuffing at him and getting a kick in whenever they got a chance.

You see, nobody had bothered to tell them that the nigger was free.

Most of the people who knowed it was still inside, or coming down the stairs, and the ones who lit out after the other mob and tried to tell them what had happened you couldn't hear in all that racket, hollering and yelling and pistols going off and scared kids and horses screaming, while dogs was barking and howling everywhere. Some of us managed to get across the street, running over the boards so as to head off the rest before they got there with the nigger, because they had already waded into the street and started towards the gallows in the shortest direction.

This slowed them down considerable, and the nigger begun to put up a good fight, on account of he had his feet under him for the first time. He was standing there up to his knees in the muck, and was slathered with it, redder than a Injun, and even though he had them chains on, his fists was pounding away like steam hammers. There was a little space cleared around him, and he kept it clear. Those of us on the other side, we jumped in too, and started to slosh our way across the street to try and tell the others what had happened, but when we got there, you couldn't tell nobody anything, because it was just one great big red pile of bodies and arms and legs, where they had jumped in and down on the nigger at last.

A couple of us had took along pieces of lumber left over from the gallows and begun to work these up and down at the pile, while the rest of us tore and clawed at the muddy arms and legs, and when the others seen what we was doing, naturally they begun to fight back, all eye-whites and teeth. It was for all the world like some goddam big red animal that had rose up out of that muck, one body and a thousand eyes and arms. One of them arms got me right in the throat, knocking me back a ways, though not too far, because the mud held like glue. I went down grabbing for air and hit something, which was the Captain, and he fell back hisself, a gone goose.

Well, that kept me from falling, and as soon as I got my balance back, I reached down and hauled him to his feet, but he shook me loose when I tried to wipe the mud off him and kept on plowing toward the pile, which had begun to move now, coming on towards the gallows. You could see the nigger now, though he was the same color as the rest of the mob, on account of being at the center of attention, so to speak, and there was wet thumping sounds and a cry every now and then coming out of the rest of the sounds, where he was still laying around with those tremendous fists. The Captain headed right for the center, waving his arm and I guess shouting. I seen he had his pistol, but it was all covered with mud from where he had fallen down, and I said to myself, Christ, I hope he don't try to use that, but he did. He pointed it above the heads of everybody and pulled the trigger.

It went off like a bombshell, but without hardly any more sound above the general commotion than a firecracker. It busted into a thousand smithereens; and the Captain just stood there, looking at his hand which was still pointed in the air, holding onto the remains of the gun.

The crowd churned right on by him, that nigger fighting every foot of the way, but getting shoved along anyhow, and the people behind who was trying to stop them, some got knocked down and some grabbed aholt of whatever they could, but none of it done any good. The Captain threw the butt of his pistol at the mob and begun to suck blood and muck off his hand, sucking and spitting and all the time plowing the best he could after the rest. I went along too, but couldn't do more than trail him, it being so hard going there in that awful slew.

The nigger had got pushed up against the gallows now, and his fists was still driving in and out, only not so fast as before, and his face was caked all over red, so you knowed he couldn't see what he was doing, not that it made much difference. Still, when Lafe Chancellor up there on the platform leaned over and brought his crowbar down, that marvelous nigger give a dodge of his head to one side, so Lafe's crow swung into his shoulder instead of his skull. The first swipe did, anyways. Lafe heisted it up again, and the second time he give the bar a side-to-side lick instead of a up-and-down one, and since the nigger was near froze with pain and stuck in the mud and hemmed in besides, Lafe got him right in the head. The crow stuck two inches in along a line twice that distance, and Lafe had to give it a little twist to get it free. The blood come out then, pumping like red water out of a red rock.

Well, that killed him, of course, and the nigger just keeled over into that little space his fists had kept cleared around him, while the crowd stood looking at him, except for them who was pushing in so they could have a look-see, too. Lafe didn't rest none from his exertions, though. He tossed the crow to one side and picked up the rope, one end of which he throwed to the men below and told them to get it round the nigger before he sunk out of sight, which they done, and then Lafe and some others hauled away. Up come the nigger until most of him was out of the mud, and even slathered all over like he was, anybody with eyes could see that the clothes had been tore off him, that there wasn't a stitch left, only just the chains.

"Jaybird nakkid!" somebody shouted, and then they all begun to holler at once, louder than ever before, and there was some women close by screeching and covering up their children's eyes except for them that fainted, and the kids without folks begun to jump up and down, shouting, "Nakkid, he's nakkid!" which they always done when they followed Anse Pulcherd out of town, and didn't know no better. By this time the Captain had got to the boardwalk, but with his one hurt hand, he couldn't pull hisself out of the muck, so I climbed up and pulled him after me.

"Find–the–boy," he said, blowing like a bellows, and then went staggering up onto the platform and laid his hurt hand on Lafe's shoulder, to keep from falling down it looked like. Lafe was still holding onto the rope, and he turned around to see who it was, and give the Captain a big grin.

"We got him," he said. "You want us to string him up anyways? The contract says . . ."

"You're–under–arrest," said the Captain, gulping air at the same time.

"What the hell you talkin' about?" asked Lafe. "Why, the son-of-a-bitch might a killed somebody if I hadn't got him first. And we was gonna hang him anyways, wasn't we?"

"No," said the Captain, still gulping air like a fish, "we weren't. You just killed an innocent man."

He stood there, half hanging onto Lafe with his bleeding hand, and looked down at the others around the platform. It was a close moment, because none of that crowd was exactly happy at the news.

"You heard that, too?" the Captain shouted, because there was still considerable noise and tussling going on, farther out from the platform. "The Judge freed the Negro. That makes you all accomplices. Every mother's son of you!"

"*Freed* him!" Lafe cried out. "Why, half of us here saw that nigger kill Jones."

"It's true, all the same," says Matt, who had just then climbed up on the platform. "The Judge set him free."

"What kind of judge would do a thing like that?" asked Lafe. "That's what I want to know!" The men down in the mud begun to chime in, seeing how the Captain had rung them in with Lafe. "What kind of justice is it when they set a nigger free for killing a white man?"

"You'll find out soon enough," said the Captain. "Come on along now."

"You goin' to stand for this, boys?" shouted Lafe. "You all know I done right!"

The fellers down in the muck around the dead nigger begun to stir about now, on account of some of the folks who had been in the courtroom come closing in, taking an arm here and there and beginning to pull and haul at them, everybody still shouting, though not so loud as before. Then some guns come out on both sides of the street, up on the boardwalks, and it did look like more trouble.

"Hold on," said the Captain. "I'm not going to press charges against the rest of you. Not yet, anyway. So simmer down."

Well, that changed things all right, and most of the boys cooled right down. Some had already seen the little gambler down in the muck, all by hisself, still dressed fit to kill, and walking back and forth, reaching down into the mud with both arms like a man groping for eels. Now there may have been eels down in that muck, God knows, but it wasn't eels he was looking for, though it was shaped like a eel, being long and fat as a sausage. He wasn't the only one that had heard the kid say the nigger had all the gold on him, and people were quick to catch on to what he was doing down there, and drifted over to help him look, neighborly-like, and quiet, too.

They found the nigger's jacket, or what was left of it, right away, and pretty soon Sturgis and Bradley come up with his britches, both having got holt of a leg each, and when they give a tug the two legs come apart, there being not much left holding them together, so they ended up with two pockets apiece. The gambler got Jones's silver dollar and a bandana handkerchief, and Bradley got his horehounds back, but that was all the wealth anybody sluiced out of that muck even though they kept looking till nightfall. As it turned out, it was the kid who had it all the time.

Well, the Captain had begun to move away down off the platform, Matt helping him along with Lafe, who started to hang back a little. "It's jest a goddam trick!" he shouted. "You all are in this with me! Ain't none of you goin' to stop them? I'm Lafe Chancellor, boys! Lafe Chancellor! I ain't never broke a law in my life!"

Well, people looked this way and that, and it was plain they felt sorry for old Lafe and maybe a bit ashamed for him, but nobody seemed ready to step forward and help him.

"You cowardly skunks!" Lafe shouted, when he seen how it was going to be. "You bastards! There ain't one among you don't owe me money, and this is the thanks I get. Shitpokes, every one of you!"

It was true enough, about the money, I mean. But it just wasn't the way to go about getting those people on his side, reminding them he had been giving them credit and little loans, at twenty per cent. A lot of men done some quick mental accounting, and seen how they might be a little more out of debt sooner than they had thought. Besides taking offense at his name-calling, too.

"Some of you get that dead man up out of there and out of sight," the Captain said. "Put him in Chancellor's store for the time being."

"Not in *my* goddam store you don't!" Lafe said, getting all blotchy, and his eyes bugging out. "I got some rights left, don't I? Ain't I got *some* rights left?"

"All right," said the Captain. "All right. But somebody get a blanket and cover him up until Grinder gets here. There are ladies about."

Most of the ladies was clustered around the platform, thick as flies, and the Captain and Matt had some trouble getting Lafe out of there. He went along, but he wasn't used to the idea yet, and had a way of holding back as he was complaining, so they had to help him along, and the ladies kept up a gabble the whole time.

While all this was going on, I'd been looking for the kid, but everybody was so slathered over with mud they looked pretty much alike, all red as Injuns and twice as mean. Then I seen the door to Lafe's store was standing open, and moseyed in to take a look around. I didn't get very far inside before I seen what I was after, but I wasn't too joyful over finding it, on account of it had one of Lafe's new twelve-gauge, double-barrel scatter-guns, with the price tag still hanging from the trigger guard.

"Here, now," I said. "Where you goin' with that thing?"

Well, I knowed damned well enough, and so did Blondie, right on past me, but turning halfway so as to keep me in line with the gun till I was the only one in the store and feeling like a standing puddle of puke. The kid was right on schedule and didn't waste no words, but pulled back on both triggers at once. The blast shook the big window in front of the store and set Blondie back onto the boardwalk, ass-end first. Lafe opened his mouth wide enough for a dentist to walk right in with pick and shovel, and would of fallen if the Captain and Matt hadn't hold of him, and then he did fall, because he was twisting around so they couldn't stop him. I thought he was screeching, too, but it wasn't him, it was the ladies around the dead nigger, because some of the shot had gone clean through parts of Lafe and peppered a number of them from behind. It didn't go in very deep, but it stung like hell, and they carried on like a picnic party that has just sat down to say grace on a nest of yellow jackets.

As it turned out, Lafe never did make much noise, for once. He was probably dead before Blondie got back up, leaving the shotgun laying on the boardwalk and just standing there, shaking all over, with a face that was red and swole up from crying, and clothes all tore and splotched with red stuff from being down there in the street trying to help that poor dead nigger. I thought the Captain would do something, or say something, but he just stood there like everybody else, looking at Blondie. It was quiet as any church. There was this big cloud of gunsmoke hanging in the air like a blob of cotton batting, and even it didn't move.

Then come that pistol shot, KA-POW-wow, racketing back and forth betwixt the storefronts, and the kid fell down again, that blond head hitting the boards with an awful thump. Still nobody didn't say a word, but turned and looked up to where the shot had come from, and seen it was the Judge who had fired it, right through the closed window of his courtroom. Then there come the last shot, KA-POW-wowing back and forth, and I wondered what in hell he was doing wasting his powder, an old Injun fighter like him, with the kid laying there stone cold dead. But of course he wasn't wasting a thing.

The Captain and me found him still sitting behind the table where he done his presiding, and only the first two or three flies of the season had got there before us. The Captain brushed them away and covered up the Judge's face with his own coat, and it wasn't because of them flies, which never bothered the Judge when he was alive. And it wasn't because of the wound, neither, which was in his chest and never did bleed much. It was just that the look the Judge had on his face when he died was one which nobody should ever have seen, not even the Captain and me, who wouldn't have if we could of helped it.

"That's awful," I said. "That's just goddam awful."

"Poor old man," said the Captain. "It was his last judgment."

"It's awful," I said. "How come he done it, Captain. How come?"

"He's at rest now," said the Captain. "Let's leave him be."

Well, we did, and I only wish he had done the same for us. It was a long time before that face stopped haunting me like some graveyard ghost. The kind of look it was was like a picture I seen one time in a book of the Captain's, poetry it was, about the sinners suffering in hell, only worse, much worse. There wasn't no artist had the guts to draw a look like that on paper. I only seen one like it once before, and it was on the face of a woman, an Injun that had just had her baby cut in two by a trooper's sabre as he rode by. Zip, like that, without warning.

We laid them out together in Lafe's store, all five of them, including Jones, and everybody went to work right away on the funeral arrangements. It was already into the afternoon, but there wasn't nobody had appetite for lunch. We all wanted them out of sight before the sun went down so we could start in forgetting the whole thing as quick as possible. The ground up on the hill was still froze hard under the top two or three inches of mud, but that didn't stop us. We just took some of Lafe's blasting powder and blew ourselves a hole which we improved with picks and shovels until it was deep enough and wide enough, while some of the others was making coffins.

There was talk of making one big box so as to save time, but most people didn't like that idea. They figured Lafe and Jones wouldn't rest easy nailed in with a nigger. Then somebody said they should bury the nigger all by hisself, but there was those who thought it was wrong to nail up two people which had killed each other, so we ended up making three boxes, one for the Judge, one for Lafe and Jones, who was nearly of a size, and a third for Blondie and the nigger. We had to use up considerable wood from Lafe's stock, but it seemed to us he wouldn't of wanted it any other way.

We was just finishing up when out come old Grinder the undertaker with the news that Blondie wasn't no boy after all. He had been cleaning the mud off the remainders so to put something halfway decent in the boxes we was making, when he come across the moneybelt full of dust. He got to prospecting on down further south and raised that which damn near made him forget about the dust, but not quite. Well, nothing to do but everybody had to crowd into the store for a free show, and it made me sick to see it. I only took one fast peep to make sure for the record, and got out of there fast. She was flat as any man in the chest, and bony, but sure enough, there it was. Or wasn't, depending on what you were looking for.

Well, goddam it, we had to knock one of them boxes back down and build two more out of it, which meant we had to use more new lumber, just because some people didn't want no white woman buried with a black. It was silly, and I said so.

"Lord knows," I said to the Captain, "they spent considerable time laying together before this."

"Yes," he said, "I imagine so," and those was his first and last sentiments on that subject.

Well, by the time we had everybody in their box to everybody else's satisfaction, it was early evening. There was torches lit and lanterns, like a political meeting almost, except nobody was shooting off their guns or their mouths. It was very damned quiet up there on the hill after we had lowered the boxes into the ground, and you could hear the torches fluttering in the wind. Nobody knew what to do next, because when there wasn't no preacher around, the Judge had done all the burying, and the Reverend Jacobs had left town as soon as the roads opened up, on account of the congregation stopped his salary in early March.

But Bradley figured out what to do, like always, and told the Captain he ought to say a few words, since that was what he drew his pay for, especially now the Judge was gone. The Captain looked at him for a minute, all whiskers and tiredness and mud, with shadows filling up the holes in his face, and then he smiled and said:

"Words!" and laughed right out loud. "I think there's been enough words said today to last this town for a century."

Then he turned and went down the hill out of the lights, leaving us up there all alone to finish our funeral the best we could. When I got back to the jailhouse he was gone from there, too, just his badge left hanging on the key ring, and he was gone from the town as well. He stayed away for quite a spell and we begun to think he was gone for good, but no, he come back eventually with that little wife he found in Oregon and her two children and a flock of sheep. He started in herding right under everybody's nose, and there wasn't a soul in town that said a cross word against him or his wife or his children or his sheep. Not so far as I ever knowed. We all figured it was his way of doing things, and the only way you could cure him was by killing him, and nobody was in the mood just at that time for killing anybody, much less the Captain, and for a long time afterwards, neither.

Lightning Source UK Ltd.
Milton Keynes UK
UKOW02f2249280814

237718UK00001B/61/A